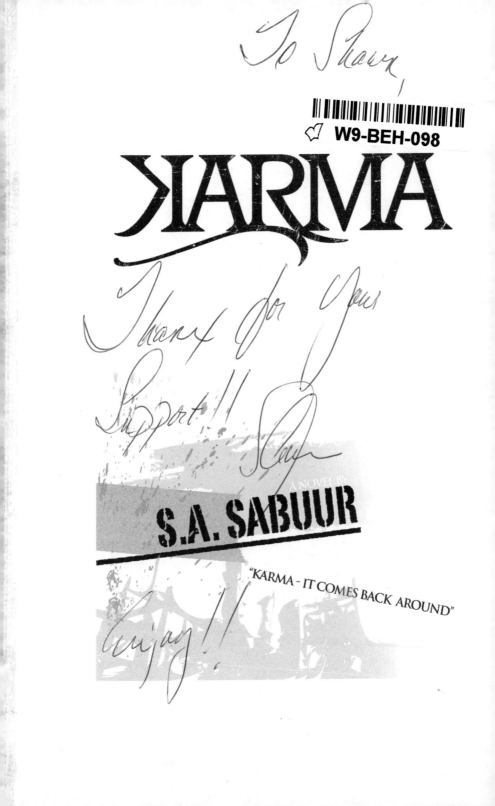

# KARMA

*A NOVEL BY*

## S.A. SABUUR

"KARMA - IT COMES BACK AROUND"

To Shaun,

Thank you for your
Support!!

Enjoy!!

# *Karma*

S.A. Sabuur

DEBORAH SMITH PUBLICATIONS

**S.A. Sabuur** is available for speaking engagements.
Contact:
Deborah Smith Publications
1 (888) 698-8486

## *Karma*

Copyright © 2005
Deborah Smith Publications

This book is a work of fiction.
Any resemblance to names, characters or incidents is entirely coincidental.

No part of this book may be reproduced in any form except
for the inclusion of brief quotations in a review, without
permission in writing from the author or publisher.

Editor:
Carla Dean

ISBN: 0-9746136-8-1

1051 Stuyvesant Avenue, #319
Union, NJ 07083
**www.deborahsmithonline.com**

In loving memory of
*Diana Faines*

# CHAPTER
# 1

## Corey:
## 7-10-86

"*Damn, another bullshit ass interview! Fuck this shit! I'm about to call my people and see if he can throw me some work. That fat motherfucker sittin' behind that desk just played me out. This is my third time this week doing this interview shit and it's my fuckin' last,*" Corey thought to himself, slamming the door to the manager's office behind him. As he walked toward the exit sign, his rage was momentarily interrupted by thoughts of his family. *"I can't keep letting them down. Shit, I can't keep letting myself down!"*

As Corey exited the warehouse, he began to realize he'd forgotten how refreshing clean air could be. Denise was going to think he'd been in a strip club all morning with the stench the manager's office left on his shirt. He walked past the loading dock and noticed there were only two Black men working on the dock out of approximately forty employees. *"Damn, they look like they're at least in their late eighties,"* he thought. He let out a sigh of relief rather than the sigh of someone who'd just been turned down for the third time this week, while wondering if that might not have been him in about another forty years.

As it started raining, Corey wished he'd watched the news last night to see what the weather would be like. Although he didn't have anything on his arms, the rain didn't seem to ease the discomfort of the one-hundred-percent humidity suffocating him. The city had been plagued with hazy, hot, and humid predictions for almost a week now, and even though everyone constantly prayed for rain, the midday shower didn't seem to make much difference. Still, there were children playing outside, hoping for some type of relief from the hellfire Mother Nature had sent them. As Corey passed by the ever so popular liquor store, he noticed the same group of thugs he used to run the streets with six years ago still standing in the same spot he'd left them in.

"C-money, what's going on?"

"What's up, fellas? You know the deal...same shit different toilet." Corey began giving his mandatory handshakes. "Where's Reg?"

"Man, that stupid nigga done got locked up again. You know his ass can't survive on the streets. He been locked up so many times he can't function when he gets out. You know what I'm sayin'? It's like the motherfucker like havin' people tellin' him what to do all fuckin' day. Shit, fuck that! Give me out here any day. You can't get no liquor in that bitch. Know what I'm sayin'?" Curtis informed him.

"Yeah, I guess so, man. So what you got planned for the day?"

"Man, I'ma finish this bottle off and enjoy this little bit of rain that we been blessed with. After that, we'll probably swing by the park and look for some bitches. Know what I mean?"

"Well..."

"Oh, my bad, man. I forgot that you don't get down

like that no more. How's the family?"

"Everybody's alright, Curt. I'm just out here trying to find some work. You know, trying to maintain."

"Yo C-money, you know it's always cake out here."

"Yeah, I know, but I got a family now. I can't be out here like that anymore. Fuck around and end up like Reg. I ain't even trying to be there, man."

"I feel you, money."

"I'll catch up with you later. Be safe," Corey said as he walked away. *"He knows damn well he needs to get his old ass off of that corner,"* he thought.

Curtis had watched Corey grow up and showed him how to take advantage of the streets. Corey knew he'd always have love for Curtis for being there, but it didn't take Corey long to realize there was nothing in the streets for him. That is, unless he was trying to invest most of his time into helping the penile system prosper, or devote himself to increasing the AIDS population. His father lived his entire life worshipping the *"easy cake"* or *"quick money"* god, and now he was a stakeholder in the federal penitentiary. Like many teenagers, Corey sold drugs as an easy way to make a few extra dollars, and not because he had to. He was never considered to be a "thug". He just knew how to handle himself. He knew the familiar outcomes of street life and chose to stay as far away from it as possible, unless he *had* to go back.

His mother blamed her chaotic behavior on the fact she couldn't cope without his father. So she went into the farming business, bought herself a *"white horse"*, and rode off into the sunset with the sick bastard who sold it to her. He hadn't seen her since, and didn't want to see her either, for that matter. It wasn't a good feeling coming home from school and…no one's home. There's nothing to eat but a couple of homegrown Chia Pets that have been sitting on a plate inside the refrigerator for three weeks. And to make it worse, you wake up the next morning and still…no one's home.

*"I just thank God my grandmother took me in when she did. I might have been another Curtis or Reg. As they say, 'If not for the grace of God, there go I.'"*

The rain stopped and the haze from the sun began to bear down on him like a flamethrower from the heavens. As Corey continued to walk home, he reminisced about his grandmother and how she would sit and talk to him about her upbringing. He had a lot of respect for her. She came up during times of segregation and spent most of her life working for just a few dollars a week. She spoke of the hardships her family endured and how she always managed to somehow keep everyone together. She was very family-oriented, the type of woman who religiously believed in Sunday dinner, Sunday prayer, and listening to gospel music all day, everyday. Corey wanted to have those same qualities with his own family someday.

His thoughts suddenly shifted to his wife, Denise. He met her when he was about fifteen and loved her from the first time he saw her. She was beautiful in every sense of the word. He still remembered the day they met, as if it were yesterday. Boys have a funny way of showing a girl they're interested in them. As she walked home from school one day, he decided to make a snowball and throw it at her for absolutely no reason. He also remembered the ass kicking she dished out to him for that incident. He still hated himself for it 'til this day.

*"What ever happened to offering to buy a girl a soda or a bag of chips?"* he wondered.

It still worked out, though. She felt bad for the shiner

she'd given him, and they eventually became friends.

Every boy in the neighborhood wanted her. This may have been partially due to the fact that she lied and told everyone she was half Black, half Hawaiian. She had the hair and eyes of one, but she wasn't. Both her parents were definitely of African descent. It's been said, though, that beauty can skip a generation or two before resurfacing. He guessed that was the case with Denise, because she was breathtakingly beautiful.

Corey never truly forgave Denise for getting pregnant by someone else her first year in college, although he told her he did. They made plans to get married and start a family after she finished her education, and even though they did, the thoughts of another man making love to her still haunted him. People say it's best to forgive and forget, but you never really forget.

Corey began to clench his teeth together and almost chipped a tooth. "Get it together, Corey. That's in the past, man," he mumbled to himself.

As he made his way around the corner and onto his street, he saw his wife sitting on the stairs of their home doing her, their, daughter's hair. Denise was one of the most intriguing women he'd ever seen. Her hair was so black, it had a bluish tint. It spiraled halfway down her back and the day's humidity gave it a fresh out-of-the-shower appearance. Her eyes were just as dark and it was hard to determine which was brighter, the whites of her eyes or her teeth. When she smiled, it was as if you could hear angels singing. Her body was perfect, flawless. You would think after just having her second child, her stomach would have many stretch marks, as if it were trying to display some type of map exhibiting different roadways, or that she'd at least be tripping over her own breasts by now. Somehow, she held onto the same beauty she had since he'd first seen her. Her skin had an eccentric complexion which provided an almost bronze, yet coffee-n-cream, effect. It wasn't hard to see how she'd gotten away with her little story about being the product of a biracial marriage when they were younger.

"Hey, sweetheart, how did it go?" she asked as he approached their stairs. A slight breeze caused her hair to gently rest partially across her face. "You don't look too happy," she said while casually moving her hair from her eyes.

"Hi, baby!" Corey said. The elation Denise had on her face from seeing him almost made him forget how terrible his day was going. "Same shit. It's almost like déjà vu. It's been three days and once again, I found myself sitting in front of some cocky, arrogant speaking bastard, waiting for him to tell me that I'm overqualified, under qualified, or that the guy who just left took the position. What the hell else am I supposed to do?"

Corey knew there were other ways of getting money, but he knew he couldn't go back to that. He had responsibilities now: Denise, Katrina, and now, Kareem. He bent over and gently kissed Denise's forehead.

"Hi, Daddy," Katrina said. Although she knew she wasn't his biological daughter, she still considered Corey her father and loved him dearly.

"Heeyy, Pumpkin," he said with a glowing smile. The sight of one of her front teeth missing caused him to giggle. "I hope you've been watching where you're running lately. I'd hate to see you knock out another tooth."

"Stop laughing at me, Daddy." She folded her arms and poked out her bottom lip as if to pretend he'd hurt her

11

feelings.

"I'm sorry, Pumpkin. You just look so cute with that tooth missing in front of your mouth. What are you eating?"

"A lollipop," she responded in a childlike tone.

"I guess you don't want the few teeth that you have left either, huh?"

"Leave her alone, baby. It's the only thing that'll keep her still long enough for me to do her hair. Tell me about your interview this morning."

"Bastard gave me every excuse not to hire me. Said I didn't have enough experience."

"What kind of damn experience do you need to pick up boxes and put them on a truck?" Denise began to feel her husband's aggravation.

"That's the same question I asked. He was a redneck anyway. I probably wouldn't have lasted. I could see me whippin' his ass the first day of work. It ain't even worth it. The pay wasn't shit anyway. You've seen his fat ass in the neighborhood before."

"I have?"

"Yeah. He drives that maroon El Dorado with the Confederate flag on the bumper. He runs that warehouse in the industrial district outside of town. It's been there for years. That racist faggot ain't got a problem coming around here to find a Black or Hispanic prostitute to suck his little pink dick, though. Somebody told me he said that was all Black and Hispanic women were good for. And he walks around here telling everybody he's a God fearing man. Give me a fuckin' break. Yet and still, I had to sit there holding down my breakfast and watch his saliva saturate the end of his cigar as he humiliated me by blowing smoke in my damn face. I swear, D, I don't think I can keep doin' this job search shit much longer. It took everything in me to keep from jumping over his desk and beating the fuck out of his 1975 Swedish-knit Christmas tie wearin' ass. The bastard must be caught in a time warp."

Denise remained momentarily silent, trying to think of what to say to give him a boost of confidence. "Well, you know the fast food place down the street is hiring."

"I told you about that shit, Denise! I ain't puttin' on no clown suit and flippin' burgers for no fuckin' body!"

"I'm sorry, Corey. It was just a suggestion. And watch your mouth around the children! You venting is one thing, but disrespecting me by speaking to me that way is another."

"Yeah well, next time '*suggest*' something else." Corey began making his way up the stairs and into their house, being wary not to fall into the gap that was present from a missing stair. "Excuse me," he said while grabbing the old, rusted, squeaking screen door and slamming it after he had entered.

There's nothing more gratifying than coming home to family, as long as there's no extra stress when you get there. He didn't have expensive furniture, but his home was still comfortable and had come a long way. The couch, grayish-brown, was made of a corduroy material and a faded floral sheet lay over it covering some of the holes that years of wear and tear had left. Since Denise recently purchased a new twenty-seven inch television set, it kind of gave the living room a more contemporary facade. The old TV had the infamous pair of pliers hanging in place of a knob that was once there and made a perfect stand for the new model that sat on top of it.

He plopped down on the couch and began reaching

under the sheet trying to locate the remote control. *"There it is, on the floor again. Katrina probably got hold of it,"* he thought silently. As he reached down to pick it up, the sticky film covering it made it apparent she'd had her hands on it. Being that close to the floor reminded Corey of just how lifeless his hardwood floors had become. As months passed by, he found himself constantly lying by saying he'd take care of it some other time.

After kicking off his shoes, Corey suddenly felt one of his socks become wet. He quickly snatched his foot from the floor and saw the scrawny, diminutive, wire-haired mutt, which Katrina begged him to keep, licking his toes. "Not now, Miles, I'm not in the mood!" His first impulse was to kick the hell out of it, but instead he gave it a gentle push with the bottom of his foot. Two days ago, Katrina found the animal under the stairs of the front porch while attempting to seek sanctuary from the heat wave. He was dehydrated, malnourished, and so dirty at the time that it was difficult to determine whether he was light brown or dark beige. At Katrina's insistent whining, Corey brought him inside and gave him water and some leftover pieces of turkey breast which he found in the refrigerator. He explained to Katrina they couldn't keep him because he probably had an owner somewhere searching for him, but she didn't care. She told him if the owner really cared, he wouldn't have lost him in the first place. Corey finally gave in.

Corey had a habit of giving in to Katrina. She was extremely intelligent for her age and this impressed him. Whatever she wanted, he gave it to her. This may have been because he knew she wasn't his daughter, so he seemed to overstress his adoration for her. He would never want her to feel he loved Kareem more than he loved her. But this exaggerated fondness caused him to spoil her and he could not see the mischievous sprite he was creating.

Corey turned on the television and began staring at it, but with all of the stress that overwhelmed him; it was more like the television was watching him. "Now what the hell am I going to do?" he said with a frustrated sigh before placing his head back and nodding off.

"Sweetheart, sweetheart, wake up." Denise stood over him with a steaming plate of spaghetti while nudging his knee with her own. "Corey, I made lunch for you."

"Huh? Oh, thanks, baby. Man, how long was I out for?"

"About three hours."

"Whoa, this smells good." Corey knew cooking was one of Denise's better qualities and perhaps the best thing her mother, Diana, could have passed on to her.

Diana was a sweet and caring older woman whom everyone in the neighborhood adored, especially the younger group of boys of which most tried to get on her good side with aspirations of dating her daughter. She was a very prominent figure in the area, having spent most of her life in that neighborhood. Everyone called her Momma Di, short for Diana, because she basically raised half of the community. She was midwife and nanny to most of the children who grew up there. Her family migrated north from the Bayou in the early sixties when being Black wasn't trendy. Since then, almost everyone in town has had the pleasure of sampling some of her famous gumbo and scrumptious jambalaya. Momma Di had a very strong impact on her neighbors and everyone respected her. She repeatedly spoke of unity within the community and headed the neighborhood watch committee. Of course, there were those who contracted the '*every man for himself*' disease, but most of the community modeled themselves around her beliefs. They had unconditional love for Momma Di, and she thrived on their heartfelt feelings for her.

"Damn, this is good, D."

"Yeah, I know… I know," Denise arrogantly boasted. She knew making pots talk was part of her forte. Although she strongly resembled her mother, she could never compare to her mother's expertise in the kitchen.

Diana was a well-built woman, gorgeous, and unique, the type of woman any man knew he would have been chasing about twenty-five or thirty years ago. Though she had to be at least sixty, her appearance was enough to make you think twice about dating "older" women. She and Denise favored each other deeply, except for Momma Di had a smile that could pierce your soul and relieve you of any hardship you may have had at that moment. Beauty was undeniably something that ran in their family, and any man who had the pleasure of spending even the smallest portion of their lives with either of them had truly been blessed.

"So, you wanna talk?" Denise asked. The genuine quality of her voice eased Corey's aggravation for a moment and he began to feel a little less tense about his situation.

"Yeah, but before we do, I wanna apologize for snapping at you earlier and cursing in front of the kids."

"Come on, Corey, you think I don't know how frustrating this job search shit is. I can tell your attitude just by looking at your facial expressions, even though you try to hide it from me." She smiled and gave him a quick, yet reassuring, peck on his lips.

"I thought I was doing a good job of keeping my feelings hidden," he facetiously replied.

"Baby, I know you better than you know yourself."

By now, her boastful smile was becoming very evident.

"Oh, so what! You ain't gotta talk shit!"

They both began laughing about the conversation, and while Corey appeared to be entertained by this discussion, he knew she was right and did not find her little sarcastic statement funny at all.

"Listen, can we talk about my day later? I wanna go and shoot a little hoop before it gets too dark outside."

"Go ahead, Corey. I know you'd probably have a conniption fit if you missed one day hanging with your boys."

"Thanks, D. Hey, where's my babies?"

"Kareem is still asleep and Katrina just went to join him about half an hour ago. Go on, you know they'll be wide awake by the time you get back here."

"Alright, give 'em love for me."

"Go give 'em love yourself. You have to go pass their bedroom to change your clothes anyway."

"Yeah, you're right." Corey took an alleviating stretch, inhaled the last of his meal, and got up to change out of the suit he was wearing. "Yo, what's up with dinner?"

"You'll see when you come home." She smiled, grabbed his empty plate, and headed for the kitchen.

Corey watched as she walked away, paying close attention to the movement of her hips. Even though he wasn't in the mood for sex, every time he saw her that tingling feeling would overcome him and he could feel a pre-erection approaching. *"Damn,"* he thought to himself and continued walking towards the bedroom.

"Hey, Denise, where'd you put my sweat socks?" Corey yelled as he fumbled through an old, olive green, military style laundry bag.

"I put them in your top drawer... where they belong!" she shouted upstairs.

Corey was known for living out of a laundry bag. It may have been because he became accustomed to constantly being on the move, bouncing from one friend's house to another before his grandmother finally got hold of him. This irritated Denise more than the fact of Corey not being able to retain gainful employment.

"I see 'em!" Corey said with a hint of frustration. He hated not being able to locate something. If *he* put it somewhere, then *he* always knew where it was. He wasn't a slob. He just had his own "personal" way of organizing his property. And that "way" usually did not correspond with Diana's housekeeping regulations.

As Corey shuffled through several pair of underwear, his hand came across a picture he set aside over a year ago. Although he *thought* his organizing skills were up to par, Corey would sometimes hide things from himself.

It was a photograph of him and his parents. He looked about five years old in the picture. He stared at it for a moment trying to figure which was funnier, the trio of Afros or the ridiculous outfits they were wearing. Butterfly collars?! And why did his father have rodents glued to the sides of his face? There was no question as to why Corey subconsciously hid this picture. It was the most embarrassing thing he'd ever seen!

"Pops," Corey whispered to himself while gently rubbing his index finger over the portrait of his father.

He missed his father more than his mother. He could not forgive her for the pain she brought him. Her weakness and lack of hunger for survival sickened him. Yes, it was clear his father had done something injudicious, but to turn to heroin as a catalyst was even more insane. Don't get it confused...Corey's father would have never received a "Daddy of the Year" award, but he had a profound love for his son and Corey sensed it. Sure, they never went to any ball games or fished on a lake together, but sometimes these things don't have any bearing when it comes to the bond between father and son.

His mother, on the other hand, gave him everything he wanted. You know, the type of woman who'd take her child with her to a supermarket and no matter what the kid threw in the shopping cart, she never broke a stride. Anything Corey wanted, Corey got. "That's Momma's little man," was her favorite saying, even when he became a teen-ager. Can you imagine the embarrassment of leaving home to play football with your friends at the age of fourteen and your mother stopping you to adjust your clothes right in front of them?! If it wasn't for the fact his grandmother got him when she did, he would have probably grown up to be another pathetic middle-aged man living in his mother's basement. Instead of showering him with tough love, she blanketed him with gold. But, remember the old saying, "You can't buy love."

Corey placed the picture under an old pair of thermals he'd forgotten he owned and continued changing into a pair of shorts and a T-shirt.

"I should be back in a couple of hours, D. Maybe we'll go catch a flick or something, alright?" he said as he headed to the front door.

"I'm not really in the mood to go out. Why can't we just take it easy here instead? I'm kind of tired, and you know I have to get ready for work tomorrow. I can't miss anymore days."

"It doesn't matter. I wish *I* had a job to miss days from," Corey mumbled in a low and slightly jealous tone.

"It'll all work out, baby," she replied as she kissed him goodbye. "I love you."

"I love you, too, sweetheart. Just work with me."

"Don't worry, I got your back." She smiled and watched as he made his way through the doors and down the stairs.

# CHAPTER
# 2

*I*t was about four o'clock in the afternoon and the heat made the temperature virtually unbearable. It gave the asphalt an almost sodden appearance. Corey began to have second thoughts about going to play ball, thinking it might be better if he reached inside himself to find his youth and play in a fire hydrant instead.

He continued down his block and turned into an alley, attempting to shorten his distance to the park. The shade from the houses made the alley comfortably cooler. However, when he exited the alley, the temperature smacked him so hard it nearly knocked him out. As he passed the liquor store, he noticed how unusually desolate it had become since earlier that day. His friends, who normally spent most of their time blocking the doorway, were gone now. You'd think they worked there from the way they opened the door for customers and helped people to their cars, hoping to obtain a tip. Although the park was only a few blocks from the house, Corey would pass four more liquor stores before getting there. His buddies may have decided to expand their business ventures to another location.

Once he reached the park, he saw three of his friends sitting on a bench enjoying a frosty six-pack of cheap beer.

"Curtis, what's goin' on?" Corey asked, already

drenched with perspiration.

"What's up, C-money? Just tryin' to stay cool," Curtis responded, as if trying to catch his breath. "You here to play ball?" he asked. A wet towel, which draped over his head, made it difficult to see his eyes.

"Yeah, I thought about it, but now I don't know. It's hot as hell out here. Mess around and pass out, then I gotta worry about one o' you ugly motherfuckers tryin' to give me mouth-to-mouth."

"Shit nigga, yo ass'll be dead before I give you mouth-to-mouth."

"Fuck you!" Corey said with a smile before punching Curtis on the shoulder. "And I told you about that C-money shit. I'm too old for that, man."

"Shut up and stop acting like a little bitch. You know I'm just teasin' you. We go back too far for your punk-ass to be catching feelings with me," Curtis replied. He knew Corey for about ten years, so this little game of tit-for-tat was just a ritual that somehow grew between them over the years.

Curtis looked at Corey as the younger brother he never had...well, did have but was one of those stakeholders mentioned earlier. He would be finishing up the rest of his career in a state penitentiary for a double homicide he committed some time ago. Another talented soul wasted. He never took any music lessons, but his drumming abilities rivaled those of Tito Fuentes.

Curtis' younger brother and Corey were close before he went to jail, so Curtis began keeping a close eye on him. He taught Corey the things he should have taught his brother, but was too busy doing his own thing at the time to do. He could see Corey was on that well-traveled road to destruction and figured maybe if he guided Corey in the right direction, God would forgive him for not guiding his own brother.

Curtis was about thirty-five years old and huge, standing at least six foot four and weighing approximately two hundred eighty pounds. He never started any trouble, but respect for a man that size was very easy to attain. He wasn't muscular, but his gut could narrate the stories of the many kegs it devoured over the years. Curtis was the epitome of a gentle giant. Although he tried to keep a short Afro, father time decided to give it a Roman Coliseum effect. Everyone tried to get him to just cut it off but, for some reason, Curtis thought the Sherman Hemsley look was the thing to have.

Corey had love for Curtis, but only wished he would get off the streets. The funny thing was Curtis *always* had money in his pocket. He told Corey he wasn't selling drugs, but he could've been lying just to make sure Corey didn't try to follow in his footsteps. If he wasn't lying, Corey sure wished he would let him in on his little secret.

Corey looked behind Curtis. "Oh, what's up, Gary? I didn't even see you sitting back there."

"Yeah, you never see me, blind ass bitch," Gary mumbled as his eyes rolled back into the top of his head and he returned to that blissful feeling he lived for.

Now Gary, on the other hand, wasn't shit and wasn't ever going to be shit because his momma and daddy weren't shit. He came from a long line of drug abusers, and when parents indulge in drugs, it usually leads to a lack of structure in the home.

Gary was the neighborhood bum and a drug addict. And from looking at the white film in the corners of his mouth, it was evident that he was high at that very moment. For the life of him, Corey could not fathom how Curtis could still hang with this idiot. Gary was the reason people locked their doors at night. He'd steal your newspaper off of your porch and sell it just to make an easy fifteen cents. There was no question about where he got *his* money. If you were missing something, Gary was getting high. If you thought an alley cat tipped over your garbage and went through it, Gary was getting high. He sold anything he could get his hands on. Once, he cut the hair off his head and testicles, then tried to sell it to a human hair donor for a couple of bucks.

Even though Corey greeted him whenever they came into contact with one another, which wasn't often, he really detested him. It was probably because he reminded him of his mother.

"Nigga, I speak to yo' ass every time I see you." Corey's retort caused Gary's eyes to open slightly, and he knew if he exchanged too many more words with Gary, this bogus conversation they were engaged in would become brutal.

Corey's beef with Gary started about four years ago during the premature stages of his relationship with Denise. One day, she informed Corey that Gary tried to snatch her pocketbook from her shoulder when she was leaving a grocery store. When he confronted Gary about it, he refuted her accusations. He claimed he thought it was falling and that he was trying to lift it back onto her arm. Even though Corey knew his story was a lie, he didn't retaliate because of the fact they grew up together. Deep down, he still wanted to kick his ass for disrespecting him.

"Corey, you talk a lot o' shit. If I wasn't fucked up right now, I'd be kickin' yo' ass nigga."

"Motherfucker, you always fucked up," Curtis interceded.

"Yeah well, if I wasn't *always* fucked up, I'd be kickin' his ass," Gary said, laughing as he slid back into his congenial doze.

"Curt, I don't know how you can still fuck wit' Gary. You need to cut his ass loose." Corey's attitude was becoming even more volatile.

"You know how I am, Corey. If I don't watch him, who will?"

"I guess I feel you, man. But you know how *I* am. If you don't give a fuck about yourself, then how can I give a fuck about you?"

"Listen, Corey, you remember what happened to my little brother, right?"

"Yeah, but…"

"No, hear me out. Sometimes these streets can really do a number on you. You can get so caught up in them that they'll cloud your ability to reason. We know that it's part of our nature as men to secure an income and take care o' shit, but it's easy to fall victim to these streets an' we start tryin' to get shit the wrong way. See, niggas got a problem. Four hundred and fifty years ago, unity was taken from us and we haven't found it since. We came to this country the same time White people did and we still ain't got shit. Latinos really just got here and they own damn near every corner store you see. The Jews run the country and the Asians is buyin' everything from them. Check out the Jamaicans and Haitians, they got the cab industry on lock. Now, I ain't sayin' that there's a problem with none of this. I just want you to tell me why is shit like that?"

"I don't know. You tell me."

"Because them motherfuckers stick together, that's why. First thing we do is sit around and talk about what the

White man is doin' to us and how he's holdin' us down. Dig man, I been in these streets for almost thirty-five years and ain't no White man ever tried to stick me up, steal my car, or break in my house. Shit, come to think about it, I hardly ever see one o' them niggas around here. That's just an excuse we use to not do what the fuck we suppose to be doin'. If we ever decided to come together, our whole situation would change. See, I know I done fucked up my life, got a record longer than yo' block, but I'ma try to make sure I watch over you younger cats and keep y'all from fuckin' yo' shit up more than it already is, alright?"

"No doubt, Curt. I never looked at this shit like that before. I appreciate you comin' at me like that, too, man. Check it out, Curt. I know you miss your brother being out here, and I miss him, too. But I just wanna let you know that you still got a little brother out here trying to make it."

"That's why I'm on you the way that I am." While Curtis was pleased to have passed his thoughts on society to Corey, his head slowly began to hang in shame. He knew he wasn't anything to be proud of. "Alright, enough of this sentimental bullshit. Are you drinkin' or what?"

"Naw, you know I don't fuck with that poison," Corey said while still displaying a look of gratitude for the knowledge he just received.

"Fuck that poison shit! It's hot as fuck out here!" Curtis yelled. As he raised his head, he caught a glimpse of Corey's eyes and noticed a tear remaining in one of its corners. This reassured him of the fact, what he said to Corey caught his attention. "It's all good, though. Ain't no love lost." He grabbed his hand and embraced him…like only a brother could.

"You know, Curt, you were right about one thing."

"What's that, lil' bro'?"

"It *is* hot as hell out here! I think I'ma take it in for the night. Come by the house if anything is happening later."

"No doubt, man. Be safe."

"Alright. Yo check you later, Gary."

Gary lifted his head for a brief moment and said, "Yeah, whatever, punk-ass motherfucker," then began to doze again, revisiting heaven.

Regardless if Gary was high or sober, he always ran his mouth. He was once a Golden Gloves champion, and even though he was about five foot ten, a hundred twenty pounds, he still possessed the ingenuity to knock out the average person if necessary.

"Always talkin' shit, Gary," Corey stated, still looking for the opportunity to take revenge for what he'd done to Denise.

Gary began to slur now and the pasty saliva running down his chin caused Corey's glands to begin producing the fluid which develops in your mouth right before you throw up. "An' I can back my shit up, too, bitch!" he sputtered.

Corey turned and began to walk away, knowing if Gary uttered one more word, it was on. "Whatever," he simply responded.

Corey wasn't a slouch, either. He also spent time in the gym and had no problem holding his own. He just didn't feel it was fair catching Gary in this condition. He wanted Gary when he was at his best. But at the rate Gary was going, chances of that happening got slimmer by the minute.

As Corey continued past the park's entrance, someone entering accidentally bumped into him. Corey turned to ask for an apology but became baffled at the sight of this person wearing a pair of black shorts, black boots, and a black hooded sweatshirt in this type of weather. Not only was the temperature close to ninety-eight degrees, but this lunatic also had the hood draped over his head! Corey watched as the bizarre character slowly made his way into the park and thought to himself, *"Some things are better left alone."*

"Curtis, can I see you for a minute!" the hooded individual shouted from across the basketball court as he made his way toward the bleachers that Curtis and Gary occupied. The tone of his voice caused Corey to pause and turn to catch a glimpse of the situation.

"Who are you? I don't think you know me, man," Curtis replied as he rose from his seat. "And I don't think I like the way that you asked to see me either, nigger."

"I don't give a fuck what you like! Payback's a bitch and revenge is a motherfucker, bitch!"

Corey listened to the conversation and casually began making his way back toward his newly found big brother. He suddenly realized the furious man, who now stood in front of Curtis, never took his hands from the pocket that was positioned on the front of his hoodie. Come to think of it, his hands had been there when he collided with Corey near the park's entrance. Corey became anxious and decided to pick up his pace. As he drew closer to the ruckus which was taking place, he could hear the man yell, "Your turn, bitch!" as he slowly pulled his right hand from the sweatshirt.

Suddenly, time stood still and Corey's stride abruptly ended. He reached out to grab the murderer who was being born right before his eyes, but quickly realized he was at least twenty feet away from him. He opened his mouth and attempted to yell, but nothing came out. Nothing came out! Nothing moved! Nothing...just the man's hand! A basketball rebounding from a backboard hovered in mid-air. A flock of sparrows passing overhead became motionless before his eyes. The entire park died, then…three shots. And at that moment there *was* no heat wave, just the cold feeling of watching a soul leave its temple. As the bullets left their home with a thunderous sound and entered their target, the park simultaneously regained its consciousness.

Corey dropped to his knees as Curtis dropped to his death, and the tears that ran down Corey's face imitated the blood that oozed down Curtis'.

"No. No, no, nooo!!" The scream which escaped Corey's lungs was enough to bring goose pimples to the most sinister heart who heard it. "Not now…not now!" he painfully cried.

The man, who so easily pulled the trigger, turned to Corey, smiled, and put the .44 caliber Desert Eagle back into his pocket. He glanced at his surroundings and began running away from the scene he created.

Corey brought himself to his feet and bolted toward the man who'd just expressed his love for him only five minutes ago. He grabbed Curtis' head from the sweltering pavement and cradled it against his accelerated heartbeat. Curtis was dead. This wasn't Ripley's Believe It or Not, and the 3-inch crater left in the back of his head attested to it. "Come on, Curt! Don't leave, man! Please…don't leave me!" Curtis was gone and nothing would change that.

Gary's high was also gone. "What the fuck? What the fuck is going on?! Who did this shit to my man? Corey, what the fuck happened?"

"Some nigga just smoked him," Corey silently mumbled. He began to experience a lack of oxygen and his words sounded like a scratched compact disk. "W-Why, Gary? W-Why?"

Gary wiped blood and skull fragments from his face which were splattered by his comrade's demise. "I think I know the motherfucker that did this shit, man. Yo, Curt brother killed his little brother, Corey! That nigga been tellin' cats he was gonna get his ass back for that shit. Oh, this shit is fucked up, man. Fucked up! I'm outta here, man. Fuck this shit!"

"How the fuck you gonna just leave him here, Gary? You can't leave, Gary!"

"Hey, no disrespect, Corey, but I got warrants and 5-0'll be here in about two seconds. I can't do no more time, C. I'm outta here, man. If you can, take my statement for me. I'm out."

"Motherfucker, I knew you wasn't shit! He looked out for us, man!"

"Yeah, but he dead now, and me hanging around and taking a chance of gettin' locked up ain't gonna change that. I loved that nigga just like you did, but I can't be here right now. I know where you live, Corey. I'll stop by your house tomorrow and find out what happened, okay?" he said as he stumbled down the stairs of the bleachers and confusingly looked for an escape route.

Gary ran top speed out of one entrance to the park as the boys in blue ran through another. They asked very little questions about the incident, ruling it another random shooting. Corey was determined to find the assailant and take revenge, but thoughts of his family made him sensitive to the term "caught between a rock and a hard place".

Corey's interview with the police didn't last long. He was told he'd be contacted if there were any further questions, but he knew he wouldn't. He watched as the coroner zipped a long plastic bag over the face of his brother. Corey wiped the sweat and tears from his face and began to exit the park for the second time.

# CHAPTER
# 3

*I*t was now about six-thirty, and the relief of another muggy day silently crept through the haze. The temperature only decreased about five or six degrees, and for a brief moment, it almost felt as if autumn was trying to work her way in. It was the middle of July and certainly felt like it. The insufferable heat scourging the city the past couple of days increased a tension that was by now legendary in most urban areas. People can only tolerate but so much under these conditions. If heat mixed with humidity didn't do anything else, it definitely intensified an already prolonged feeling of exasperation. People normally attain a "don't speak to me, don't touch me" attitude during this time of the year.

Corey began making his way home, trying hard to hold back the tears the day's incident brought. He continued past the shortcut he chose to utilize earlier. Since the temperature had slightly declined, there was no reason for him to head in that direction. He paused for a moment just before passing the liquor store Curtis often occupied before his tragedy and could do nothing else but break down and cry.

Curtis' life was routine. He would leave his house everyday between eleven and twelve o'clock, meet with his friends, and have a few beers with them. He never caused trouble in the community. Why did God punish him for the sins of his brother? Corey began wondering how he would explain this to Curtis' ten-year-old daughter or to his girlfriend for that matter. Maybe he would ask Denise to explain it to them so he wouldn't have to.

Corey looked at his watch and realized his wife must be preparing dinner now. He then tried to figure a way to tell her what just happened at the park. He knew he'd just eaten not too long ago, but with Denise's culinary expertise, that didn't matter. It's almost like eating dinner on Thanksgiving. The food is so delectable, regardless of how full you get, you continue to stuff your face. He then questioned if he was even in the mood to eat.

"Damn, how the hell can I think about eating with all this shit going on?" he asked himself as he neared the corner of his street.

He entered his block and observed some of his more elderly neighbors sitting on their porches, which didn't surprise him. Most of them would come outside between seven and eight o'clock every evening to sit in their wicker or rocking chairs and gossip as the sun embarked on its journey beyond the horizon. He passed Mrs. Baker's house and could hear her and her friend Mrs. Green talking about Mr. Taylor who lived across the street. Corey glanced at Mr. Taylor's house and saw him listening to his granddaughter tell him how she'd just seen a man get shot at the park. She leaned forward with her hands on her knees, breathing as if she'd just run home from the park.

Next door from Mrs. Baker's house, Mr. and Mrs. Douglas sat reading their mail, discussing how pitiful the mailman was.

"Hey, Corey, did you get your mail today?"

"I'm not sure, Mrs. Douglas. I haven't checked

yet," Corey replied, although he wasn't in the mood for a conversation. "Why the hell does she have to talk so damn loud anyway?" he thought to himself as he passed their house.

"Why don't you mind your damn business, Margaret? Did you ever stop to think that maybe the boy don't want you knowing about his affairs with his mail?" Mr. Douglas said angrily while pushing his dentures back into his mouth.

"Oh, shut up, Henry! I was just trying to make conversation with the boy!"

"Well, maybe he don't wanna have a conversation with you. You ever thought about that one, Margaret, huh?"

"Just mind your business, Henry!" she snapped.

"I'll mind mine when you learn to mind yours!"

Corey let out a brief sigh of frustration and continued making his was home. "Goodbye, Mr. Douglas…Mrs. Douglas."

"Goodnight, boy," they replied in unison.

"You alright, son?" Mr. Douglas curiously asked.

"Yes," Corey replied, "I'll be alright."

This routine scenario entertained Corey. Everyday he would observe his lifeless neighbors sit outside and talk about each other. What's ironic is that they were all friends. Most of them lived in the same houses for years and had become well acquainted with each other. What amused Corey wasn't the way they talked about each other, but how they would smile and pretend they liked one another when they congregated *with* each other.

As he approached his house, he began to notice how dark its interior was. "Shit, the electric company got me!" He knew the bill was past due, and now his chaotic day just became a bit more disturbing.

He entered the house. "Denise...Denise?" The silence made him wonder if something happened. "Denise!" He passed through the hallway and flipped a light switch on his left. The bulb's illumination temporarily eased his suspicions. He noticed a wavering light emanating from his dining room. He approached it and noticed Denise standing in the doorway. She adorned herself in a red silk negligee, red lace garters, and black fishnet stockings. He could see she prepared an elegant dinner and had a great deal more planned for the evening than what was apparent at that time.

There is nothing more pleasurable than coming home to a candlelit dinner with your mate, male or female, who's waiting impatiently while wearing an erotic outfit, dying to ease the stress of your long and hectic day.

"Sit down, sweetheart," Denise whispered. The flame of a candle danced within her dark, stimulating eyes.

"What's this for?" Corey asked, caught totally off guard.

"Because I love you," she softly whispered in his ear while gently massaging his lobe with her tongue.

"Need I remind you that I *didn't* get the job today?"

"It doesn't matter. You told me about your day and now I'm gonna make you forget about it. Just sit down, relax, eat your dinner, and prepare for dessert. I'm in control now."

"Well...my day has become a lot more complicated since we last spoke." Corey tried to keep his composure but could not hold back the tears that emanated in his eyes.

"What's wrong, baby. Did something happen?" Denise asked, terminating her feeling of lust, momentarily.

"Somebody shot Curtis at the park."

"Is he gonna be all right?" she asked, stunned by his

statement.

"No, baby, they killed him right in front of me."

"Oh my God, Corey, I'm so sorry. Are you okay?"

"I'll be alright. I just don't believe this is happening. He was a good brother, you know. He did some fucked up shit in his life, but he never hurt anybody."

"Who killed him, baby?"

"Gary said it was some cat that was the older brother of one of the guys that Curtis' little brother killed. I don't understand why Curtis didn't better prepare himself for retaliation. Gary said the guy had been telling people he was gonna get revenge for his brother."

"Corey, you know these streets. I loved Curtis, too, but you know that he was no angle. He and his brother had enemies, and you know he's been on these streets all of his life. You don't know the dirt he may have done before he met you. I believe in karma. The evil you do in life will eventually come back to haunt you. I'm truly sorry for what happened to Curtis, but you, Katrina, and Kareem are all that matter to me right now. Baby, nothing matters but us, and you'd better start realizing that. Curtis is gone and will be missed, but you have a family to take care of and a wife that loves you more than you'll ever know. Now, I want you to sit, eat this dinner I prepared for you, and try to put this entire day behind you. Do you understand me?" she commanded.

"I'll try, D. Listen, I know what you're thinkin', but I ain't goin' back into these streets to jeopardize everything I've been trying to build. I told you before, that street shit is over and it would take a lot more than the death of a friend for me to pull another trigger."

"I'm glad you look at us like that. Now, I refuse to let this incident depress you more than you've already been. So, unless you want trouble here, you'll do as I said and enjoy your evening."

"Oh, it's like that now, huh?" Corey was impressed with the dominating guise Denise portrayed.

"That's right. It's like that. Now shut up and eat your dinner before you ruin the moment and ruin the dessert that I have planned for you."

Denise wasn't being selfish, but her family meant everything to her and she refused to let anything, including best friends, come between them.

Corey sat and indulged himself with the tantalizing meal his wife placed before him. Denise watched as he finished the last of his meal, then walked over to him, turned his chair to the side, and positioned herself between his legs. She then began taunting him with seducing kisses on his neck, his chest, his stomach, and his...

# CHAPTER
# 4

# Denise:
# 7-11-86

*D*enise's eyes began to squint as the sun's rays peeked through the Venetian blinds positioned above their headboard. She stretched and slowly opened one eye in an attempt to get a glimpse of the alarm clock that sat on the nightstand beside Corey.

"Oh my God, it's nine o'clock!" she yelled as she sat up. "I'm late...again!"

The commotion woke Corey and he began to mumble as if talking in his sleep. "What's wrong, honey? What are you yelling about?"

Denise jumped out the bed and stumbled over one of Corey's sneakers. "Shit! Where did I put my pants?"

"What are you doing, Denise?" Corey asked, now becoming aggravated with all of the noise she was creating.

"I'm sorry, Corey. I'm running late again. Would you mind helping me get the kids ready to go to my mother's?"

"What the hell are you talkin' about Denise? It's Saturday! Now calm down and get your butt back in the bed before you really wake the kids."

"Saturday?" She paused to think for a minute, then realized she'd taken the past two days off from work. The day felt more like Monday than Saturday to her. "Man, what the hell was I thinking? I'm sorry I woke you, baby. I kinda lost track of the days."

"Whatever. Just keep it down," he grunted.

Denise knew Corey was not a morning person. Some days he would wake up with an attitude for no reason. She never understood it, just learned to ignore it. Corey didn't have much, but Denise was crazy about him. Although he had certain habits she didn't agree with, she loved every bone in his body. She smiled and marveled at the way the sun caused the sweat on his back to glisten. It reminded her of a lake her father would take her to once a month when she was a child. He loved to fish there and would always take her with him.

Denise's childhood wasn't as complex as Corey's. Her parents were together for forty-three years before her father passed. When he died, she was already mature enough to better deal with his death. If you looked up the words "daddy's little girl" in the dictionary, there would be a picture of Denise smiling beside it. Although her father didn't spoil her, he gave her the best of everything: the best schools, the best clothes,
the best shoes, you name it. Sometimes this caused problems for her and Corey because she still wanted the best, and although he wanted to give it to her, he couldn't afford it.

Denise was the "*rich*" kid in the neighborhood. Her family lived what some like to call ghetto-fabulous. That's when you buy expensive cars, clothes, and jewelry, but don't have enough sense to take that same money and move into a better neighborhood. We see it all the time. Eighty thousand dollar Mercedes parked in the project's parking lot or buying hundred dollar boots with your welfare check. It's all the same. Denise never had to endure the hardships of "government assistance" thanks to a Bachelors' in business administration. Contrary to her upbringing, she had no intentions of spending the rest of her life in the hood.

"Are you coming back to bed, Denise?"

"No. I'm going to make breakfast. What do you want to eat, honey?"

"Nothing, really," he mumbled. "I'm not hungry yet."

"You're not hungry yet? It's nine o'clock. I'm starving."

"Baby, you know I can't eat this early." The word early sounded more like "earl" as Corey fell back asleep.

"Yeah, I love you, too, baby," she replied with a smile. She continued standing over her husband, admiring his physique while paying close attention to how their blue satin sheets rested seductively near the lower part of his back, slightly revealing part of his muscular ass.

"I have one quick question, Corey."

"What now, D?"

"Yesterday I mentioned getting up for work this morning and you didn't say anything. Why is that?"

"Maybe it's because I don't know your work schedule. I figured it may have been overtime or something. I don't know! Can I just get a little more sleep, please?"

"Whatever, sleepyhead," she replied before tossing a pillow onto his head.

What was it about this man, she wondered. He *was* extremely handsome, but didn't have a dime to his name, though. He had a body most women could only dream of holding: broad shoulders, a thick chest, and a washboard stomach which almost made you want to wash clothes. Unlike Curtis, Corey *did* bear a baldhead. His thin sideburns, which connected to his goatee, were kept so crisp you could almost cut yourself if you touched them. Corey didn't drink or smoke and Denise always complemented him on how straight and clean his teeth were. As her eyes traveled along his Adonis-like body, she remembered what his best feature was. I mean, what woman wouldn't appreciate nine and a half inches of ecstasy lying beside her every night.

She thought back to the first day they met. She didn't mean to punch him in the eye, but he had it coming to him. She never told him, but she already had a crush on him before that incident ever took place. She would secretly peek out of her window and watch him leave his house on his way to school each morning. She remembered laughing each time she saw his coke-addicted mother rush to the porch with sunglasses on attempting to adjust her son's attire. Corey's mother never realized how many of her neighbors were already up and about at five a.m. when she'd try to sneak into her house. Everyone knew how embarrassed Corey was by this, but they never mentioned anything to him concerning his mother's behavior. Still, Denise loved him with all of her heart and soul and wouldn't let him go for the world.

The thoughts of her husband suddenly caused her juices to begin flowing. She climbed back into bed hoping to arouse him to the point that he'd realize and respect her presence.

"Corey, you awake?"

"I wasn't, but if you keep doing what you're doing with your hand, I will be."

"There's more where that came…" a knock at the

bedroom door abruptly ended her seductive reply. "Come in!" she snapped. Her irritation was dreadfully evident.

The door slowly opened. "Mommy, I'm hungry," Katrina said while yawning and rubbing her eyes.

"Katrina, your timing is impeccable," Denise responded in a scolding tone.

"It's okay. Baby, handle your business," Corey said, knowing that he could've used another five minutes or so of sleep. "Maybe we can finish where we left off when the kids take their naps."

"Go wash your face and brush your teeth like Mommy showed you, Pumpkin. Mommy'll be there in a minute, alright?"

"Okay, Mommy."

"I'll finish with you later, Corey."

"Yeah, well, you know my motto, Denise. Don't start none, won't be none."

"Well, I'm startin' some so it can be some, sexy," she said as she tossed the soft sheets from her body.

"I'm ready when you are," Corey replied as he rolled over and pulled another pillow over his head. Then, he lifted his head for a moment. "By the way, honey, thank you for last night."

"Just doing my job, baby." Denise opened her closet, grabbed her robe, and made her way to an adjacent bedroom to check on Kareem. As she approached her children's room, she could hear the babbling of an energized baby opposite a partially opened door. She pushed it open and was not surprised to see her son standing in his crib taunting her with gentle bounces. He displayed an expression of absolute bliss over the sight of his mother. "That's Mommy's boy," she said as she reached to take him up into her arms. "My God, your diaper is soaked. Too much to drink last night, huh?"

"Corey!" she shouted over her shoulder. "I need you to change Kareem's pamper so I can make breakfast."

"Now?" he asked from their bedroom in an aggravated tone.

"Yes, now. He's dripping wet and I can't do everything myself. A little help would be nice."

"Alright, alright, I'm coming." As much as he didn't want to get out of bed, he knew he and Denise had an agreement to share *all* of the responsibilities in their home. He was still depressed over yesterday's incident and planned to stay in bed most of the day and mourn. He slowly extended his hand to the floor and began searching for the old, gray shorts he wore the day before. As he entered the hallway, he experienced a sharp blow to his thigh. "Ow!" he yelled as he looked down to grab his leg. "Katrina, what did I tell you about running through the house!"

"Sorry, Daddy," she replied, obviously embarrassed.

"It's not funny, girl," he scolded as he reached to pick her up to see if she'd been hurt. "Are you alright?"

"Yes," she answered while rubbing her forehead.

"You're not gonna be happy until you seriously hurt yourself," he told her before moving her hand to kiss where she was rubbing. "Come help Daddy change your brother's diaper, okay?" He really didn't want her help, but he decided to use this opportunity to keep a watchful eye on her.

Corey entered the children's room. "Hey D, I got him," he informed her.

"Thank you." She then kissed him and Katrina before asking, "What happened to her?"

"She was running through the house, as usual, and ran into my leg. She's okay."

Denise gave her an admonishing look. "We told you about running, didn't we? You're gonna hurt yourself one day, Katrina."

"I spoke to her already, Denise. Go ahead. I'll take care of these two." He looked at Kareem and began smiling. "See the stress you give your mamma."

"It's not just him, you know. Katrina's no angel, either," she said as she turned to make her way downstairs to the kitchen.

"Not my baby," Corey whispered to Katrina. "You know you my angel." He nuzzled his nose into her neck and began shaking it swiftly. This always made Katrina laugh.

"I heard that, Corey. I told you about spoiling her."

"Oops, I thought Mommy was gone already, Pumpkin," he said while lowering her to the floor.

Corey turned to pick up Kareem and place him on his back. "And what have you been up to, lil' fellow? Besides ruining another set of sheets, of course. Pumpkin, pass Daddy a diaper for your little brother, please."

As Corey removed the soggy clothes his son wore, Kareem looked at his father and began his renowned babbling as if trying to explain why he was so wet.

"What you talkin 'bout, man? I hope you're not telling me that you're about to piss in my face again."

"Yuck, Daddy! He peed in your face before?" Katrina asked while giggling at Corey's statement.

"Once, Pumpkin, but never again…I hope," he replied before joining in on her laughter.

"All done, dude. C'mon, let's see what Mommy's making for breakfast," Corey said as he tucked them under his arms. Some children find it amusing to be transported around as if they were a football.

They entered the kitchen just as Denise hung up the telephone.

"Who was that this early, Denise?" Corey inquired.

"My mother, of course. She wants us to come to dinner tomorrow evening."

"Tomorrow evening? Shoot, I'll be there tomorrow morning. You know how much I love your mom's cooking, D."

"I thought it was my cooking that you were so crazy about," she said as if disappointed by the way he praised her mother.

"You know how I feel about your cooking, D," he replied while putting the children in their highchairs. He then eased behind Denise, embraced her, and began gently kissing her on the back of her neck.

"Oh, I thought you were trying to tell me that you wanted to make your own breakfast this morning," she sarcastically replied. "And stop, Corey! You know the children are watching."

"So? Are we supposed to be keeping the fact that we love each other away from them?"

"No, but you're wearing gym shorts, and *that's* what I don't think they need to see. I can feel you poking me through my robe. Now stop it, Corey," she said before giving him a gentle tap on the back of his hand.

"Okay, okay, can you just give me a second to recover?"

"Just recover quickly before I burn these pancakes."

# CHAPTER
# 5

*A*fter breakfast, Corey and Denise decided to walk to the park where Curtis was slain the day before and pay their respects. Corey knew there would be some sort of shrine built in Curtis' honor and decided to bring a picture he and Curtis took a few years back to place on it.

Denise decided to give the children a quick birdbath. For one, she had just given them a full body bath the night before, and secondly, she knew they'd be filthy again the moment they got to the park. Denise's mother chastised her many times about not "letting the kids be kids." Denise hated seeing any dirt on them. Even when they played outside, she had no problem interrupting their playtime to wipe the smallest amount of dirt from them. She was very proud to have two beautiful offspring and would show them off as if they were million-dollar thoroughbreds every chance she got. She wanted to raise them the way she'd been raised. You know, the *best* clothes, the *best* shoes. Of course, the best to Denise meant name brand only. Remember the term *'ghetto-fabulous'?*

After dressing the kids, Denise walked down the hallway and opened a small closet that existed near the front door to retrieve Kareem's stroller. Just as she commenced to pull it from behind a shoe rack, someone began knocking at the screen door. She stood to open it.

46

"What the hell do you want?" she asked after opening it. Her tone was not at all inviting.

"I'm sorry for knockin' on your door, Denise, but I need to see Corey for a minute."

"For what?" she yelled.

"He asked me to stop by today so we could discuss what happened to Curtis yesterday," Gary said. His head hung in disgrace for what he did to Denise years ago, and guilt tortured his soul for running away from Curtis' shooting yesterday.

"Wait a minute," she said before slamming the door in his face. She knew Gary was good at what he did and could have probably packed half her house into a moving truck before Corey returned to the door.

Denise yelled down the hall, "Corey, the door!"

Corey approached her with one shoe still untied and asked her who was at the door. She whispered in a low, furious voice, "It's Gary. Why is that crackhead at our door, Corey?"

"I asked him to stop by," he replied. "I don't think that now is the time for him and me to be at war with each other."

"I understand that, Corey, but sometimes you forget that you don't live here alone. You have a wife and two small children here, also. I don't feel safe around him, and I don't want the children around him, either."

"I know who lives here, D, and you know that I'm not gonna let anything happen to any of you."

"Yeah but what about when you're not here? I don't want Gary thinking he can just stop by whenever he feels like it."

"Well, after I speak to him, I'll tell him not to meet me

here anymore. Now, can I get the door, please?" he said as he attempted to step around her.

He knew Denise was right...again. She usually was and he hated it. Normally when they had similar conversations, he would make excuses for his actions, but today he couldn't muster the energy for it. He knew energy was one of the things women had over men. A wise man once told him, "We're physically stronger than them, but they dominate where energy is concerned." This usually kept him from arguing with her. He knew he couldn't compete.

"Go ahead," she said with a satisfactory expression on her face. This was her way of acknowledging another victory.

"Thank you," Corey responded as he reached around her to open the door.

"What's up, Gary" he said as he stepped onto his porch, being mindful to close the door behind him and not expose his few possessions.

"Hey, Corey, listen, I know it's a little early, but I need to talk with you for a moment."

"I'm listening."

"You know, yesterday really messed my head up, man. I been out here for a long time and I know a bunch o' niggas that done lost their lives to these streets. But I ain't never had nobody get blown away right in front o' me. That shit's been fuckin' with me all night. You know what I'm sayin'? Made me start realizing how short this life shit is. I done some fucked up shit to a lot o' people, and I don't know how I'ma make things right. But what I do know is that it's time for me to get my shit together. Think I'ma go to one o' them twelve-step programs. Turn my life around, you know? Curtis tried to get me to go to one, but getting high was easier and gave me more pleasure. I'm not just going for myself, but I think I owe it to Curt. He was a good brother, you know. Listen man, I ain't gonna take up no more o' your time. You and me was cool at one time, man…hope we can be like that again one day."

"I feel you, Gary, and I hope you're sincere about what you're sayin'."

"I am, man. Yo, Corey, do me a favor."

"What's that?"

Gary briefly reminisced about his past and his eyes began to swell. "Apologize to your old lady for me. That was them drugs talkin'. I would tell her myself, but I know she ain't tryin' to hear that shit right now. I never meant to hurt her. And make sure you keep tryin' to do the right thing by your family. I admire you for that 'cause I ain't got one, alright?"

"No doubt, Gary. They're my life, man."

"Guess I'll see you in a couple o' weeks. Take care of yourself, Corey."

"Be easy, Gary."

Corey turned to open his door just as Denise and his children were coming out. "You guys ready?" he asked.

"We're ready," Katrina responded as he picked her up.

"And what did *he* want?" Denise asked while pushing Kareem through the doorway as he reclined in his stroller.

"Talked about going to rehab. Said he was sorry for what he did to you a few years ago," Corey said, taking a long step over the missing stair.

"Do you believe him?"

"Yeah. For some reason, I felt he was telling the truth. You could see it in his eyes. My father always said a man's eyes don't lie." Corey turned to help her carry the stroller over the missing stair. "I gotta fix this one day," he said as he looked down.

"Corey, you say that about everything. Anyway, if you believe he was telling the truth, I guess I can forgive him. Besides, life's too short to hold grudges."

"You're right. I'm glad I didn't have any grudges with Curtis," he added as he looked toward the heavens. He hoped that Curtis was listening. Then he thought about the life Curtis led and pondered on some of the other things people said he did. He began to wonder if he should have been looking up or down when he made his comment.

# CHAPTER
# 6

$\mathcal{C}$orey and his family entered the playground and, just as he thought, most of the neighborhood was gathered around the bleachers placing flowers, pouring liquor, and chatting about what a good person Curtis was. Corey spent most of his life in this neighborhood but only recognized about fifty percent of the people who spoke of Curtis. He casually made his way to the bleachers to greet some of his friends and pay his respects.

"Corey, I'll let you handle your business," Denise said as she kissed his cheek. "I see some of my girlfriends by the swings with their kids. If you need me, I'll be with them."

"Okay, Denise. You know where I'm at," Corey said as he released her hand.

As Denise approached the play area, she could hear one of her friends speaking about the incident that took place there less than twenty-four hours ago.

"Yeah, well, you know what they say. What goes around comes around. If he hadn't been in the streets with the rest of his hoodlum friends, this would have never happened."

"No, fuck that, Tina. You always tryin' to dis one of the brothers. Just 'cause he spent most of his time in the streets don't mean he was a criminal. You know Curtis had love for everybody. I don't believe you just said some ignorant shit like that, girl. That's real fucked up."

"What are you crying for, Michelle? You act as if he was your boyfriend or something. Or could it be because you and Curtis act just alike. Look at you, forty in your hand and bandana on your head. You need to get out of that ghetto mentality that you're stuck in."

"Ghetto mentality? What, I guess that I should act like you, Ms. 'I wish I were White'? The ghetto's been my life for twenty-three years and I ain't changing for nobody, especially your sell-out ass," Michelle said, wiping the tears from her face and trying to regain her composure.

"First of all, just because I decided to further my education does not mean I'm a sell-out. I have more knowledge about Black History than you ever will. Secondly, because you live in the ghetto does not mean you have to *be* ghetto. Do you plan on spending the rest of your life in this hellhole? I don't. I'm on the first thing smoking as soon as I save enough money. You can keep this crap."

"Well, ladies," Jackie interceded, "it's hard for me to get away from here. Raising six kids by yourself ain't easy."

"Damn Jackie, maybe if you keep your fuckin' legs closed you won't have that problem," Michelle snapped, astonished Jackie could have made such a ridiculous statement. "I mean, shit, what do you have now, like five different baby daddies? And what the fuck you mean raising them by yourself? You on welfare, hoe! Oh, my fault, you got *six* baby daddies. I forgot Uncle Sam," Michelle said as she began the obnoxious laugh that everyone hated so much. It may have been because of the dull, brown gold tooth she wore that became visible each time she opened her mouth and that caused her listeners to want to puke.

"Forget you, Michelle! You just mad because no

one will fuck your ugly ass. There was love in all of my relationships. Things just never worked out, that's all."

"Yeah, they *loved* to fuck you and leave you!" Michelle said while reaching out to offer Tina a high-five.

"How many more times are you going to find *love* before you give up, Jackie?" Tina asked in a somber tone. "I gave up on men a long time ago. I make more than half of them out here anyway. Plus, I have toys at home that take care of the rest."

They all began laughing at Tina's vain remarks just as Denise took a seat on the bench beside them.

"Why is it every time I see you guys, you're talking about men or sex?" Denise asked with an expression of disgust on her face.

"Oh hey, girl", Tina said. "Actually, *they* were talking about men. I was talking about masturbating," she whispered, being mindful of the children's presence.

"You're so silly, Tina," Denise said, tapping her on her thigh. "How have you been? I haven't heard from you in a while."

"I've been putting in a lot of time at the law firm. I've only been there for three months, but I want to get recognized quickly."

"That's right. Congratulations, girl," Denise said as she embraced her longtime friend. "I did hear that you passed the bar exam a few months ago."

"Thank you. I told you I wouldn't stop until I became partner of a large firm, and I meant it."

"Well, I'm proud of you. Keep at it, alright? I know you'll make it someday."

"How about you? How's married life treating you?" Tina inquired.

"It has its ups and downs, I suppose, but I'm enjoying it. You know how much I love Corey, and I don't plan on letting him go anytime soon."

"Yeah, I know," Tina interjected hoping Denise wouldn't begin her "how much I love Corey" chronicle again. "I always knew you two would be together. By the way, where *is* your knight in shining armor?"

"Over there with his friends," Denise said, pointing toward the bleachers.

"How is he holding up? I know they were best friends."

"It's got him a little messed up. I've been trying to show him that I'll be there for him, but I don't know if it's helping to ease the pain of his loss," she said as she looked across the playground at her husband.

"Do you think he's gonna try to retaliate against Curtis' killer?" Michelle asked.

"I don't know. He hasn't spoken much about it. I hope he doesn't do anything stupid. Sometimes, I wish he'd talk more when he has things on his mind."

"Denise, you know no matter how hard we try, we can never truly be their friends. They know this, but they still try to pacify our desire by deceiving us into believing we're one of their buddies. We can drink all the beer and watch all the football games we want, but we'll never be 'one of the guys'. I need a man to be my best friend as well as my lover. I think that's why I gave up on men, because they couldn't give me what I needed. Wait, let me rephrase that. I sound like a damn lesbian. I gave up on relationships is what I meant to say. Hold on to yours, Denise. There aren't many like him left, and someone lonely, such as me, would love to get her hands on him," Tina jokingly stated with smile.

"Please, Tina, as beautiful as you are? You could have any man you want."

"I know. I was just kidding."

Everyone thought Tina would have become a super model. She was almost six-feet tall and very slim. Her complexion was very dark and she possessed long, silk like hair. Her eyes were light brown, which wasn't common for someone her tone. She had always been a tomboy and this deterred boys from having any interest in dating her, along with the fact that she could run circles around them on the basketball court. Tina had it all: beauty, athleticism, and intelligence, which is probably how she attained her "I don't need a man" mentality.

Denise leaned forward to look to the right of Tina. "Hey, Jackie. Hey, Michelle."

"Damn bitch, I thought we were invisible or something," Michelle said before swallowing the last of her beer. "Where's, Pumpkin? You know I gotta see my girl."

"She's in the sandbox playing with Jackie's daugh… Katrina, come here! Come here right now!"

Katrina quickly looked at her mother, startled that she'd seen what she did, and began running toward Denise with a look of innocence on her face.

"Why did you kick that little girl, Katrina?"

"She wouldn't give me the toy."

"It's her toy, Katrina! You know better than put your hands, or feet for that matter, on other people," she said as she slapped Katrina on her shoulder. "Now go and tell her you're sorry, and keep your hands to yourself."

Katrina began crying, but instead of going to apologize to Jackie's daughter, she ran in the opposite direction towards Corey.

"What's wrong, Pumpkin?" Corey asked, surprised that she was alone.

"Mommy hit me on my arm," she answered, pointing to the spot she'd been hit.

"What did you do for her to hit you?"

"Nothing. I was playing with my friend," Katrina answered. She knew what she'd done was wrong, but she also knew Corey wouldn't chastise her for it.

"It's alright. Just stay with Daddy for now."

Denise stared across the park shocked at what she'd seen. She turned to Tina and said, "I told him about spoiling her. He should have hit her on the same spot that she was pointing to and sent her back to me. He's gonna ruin her, I swear. But I'll deal with it later because now is not the time."

Denise turned and looked back to Jackie. "Sorry, girl, I told her about that before."

"It's alright, Denise. They're just kids, you know. My daughter will be okay."

"So how's everything been?"

"All right, I guess. I've been seeing this guy for the past few months now. He has a well paying job and he really loves the kids."

"Oh God, here we go again! I guess this'll be baby daddy number seven, huh?" Michelle shouted as she rolled her eyes at Jackie. "Damn, girl, when you gonna quit?"

"Mind your business, Michelle. It's not like that with this one." Jackie directed her attention back to Denise. "He kind of reminds me of Corey, Denise. He's handsome, has his own place, and spends a lot of time with my children. He loves spending money on them, but buys too much junk food, though. I guess that's why they like him so much."

"Spends money? I never heard you say that one before," Michelle said as she stood from the bench. "Maybe this *is* the right one. Any man that'll take care of you and all them kids must be in love with you. I'm going to the store. Anybody want anything?"

"What store are you going to?" Denise asked.

"The liquor store, of course. I need another forty. And I wanna grab some chips and juice for all these kids y'all got."

"I'm okay," Denise replied. "Thanks anyway."

"Me, too," Jackie added.

"I'll take a fruit punch," said Tina.

"And I'll take a dollar, bitch," Michelle snapped with a grin.

"Here, girl, I was going to pay for it anyway."

"I was just fuckin' with you, Tina. Damn, you done got so high and mighty with them White folks you can't take a joke no more."

"Whatever, Michelle," Tina snapped back.

Tina watched as Michelle made her way out of the park. "Why does she have to act so ignorant? She was all right when we were coming up. I wonder what the hell happened."

Denise grabbed Tina's hand. "Sometimes that happens when you come from a broken home. You know her mother passed when she was young and her father couldn't really spend time raising her. He had to pay the bills and take care of the family, so he held down two jobs."

"But she didn't have to end up like this. Corey came from a broken home, too, but he turned out to be a good brother. We all remember what his mother was like. She wasn't there for him, either."

"Yeah, it doesn't have the same effect on everyone, I guess. Let's not forget that Corey's grandmother, God rest her soul, stepped in at the right time to straighten him out."

Jackie was right about one thing, and that being, Michelle was not the attractive one. She only did her hair when she went to work, and even then it was simply pulled back into a ponytail. Her teeth looked as if they hadn't been brushed since birth, and the few men that did have sex with her, most of them drunk, recalled her needing a douche or two. No one appreciated her tough demeanor, but she never started any trouble, so people tolerated her. Those who really knew her were aware of the fact that her toughness was just an act used to acquire attention.

Jackie, on the other hand, was just the opposite: very light skinned, very pretty, and very voluptuous. Some of her previous partners would go around joking about how they would sit an ashtray on her ass and smoke a cigarette when they had sex with her from behind. Although she held the title of town slut, Jackie was an extremely kind young lady. She just had a problem falling in love with every man that she met. Some say this happens due to the lack of love from a father, or father figure, at a young age. There were also rumors that her uncle had molested her since age eleven. Even though it was never validated, that's where they placed the blame for her promiscuity.

"I'll be back. I'm going to see how Corey's doing," Denise said.

"He's alright," Tina replied. "Give him some space, girl."

"Actually, I'm going to get Katrina. She doesn't need to be around all of those people drinking, sobbing, and smoking weed."

"You're right, Denise. You can leave Kareem here. I'll watch him until you come back."

"Thanks, Tina."

"Damn, Denise, what's up with this stroller?" Tina said, staring at its wheels.

"Nothing. It used to be Katrina's."

"Well, since I missed your baby shower, I'll get him a new one this week."

"You don't have to, Tina. He's fine."

"No, believe me, girl, I have to," she said, shaking her head in disappointment.

As Denise crossed the playground, she caught a glimpse of what appeared to be a large, elderly woman wearing a wide brimmed hat, leisurely entering the park while leaning on a cane for support.

"Momma," Denise whispered to herself in an uncertain manner. She paused and watched as the figure neared the bleacher area. "What am I thinking? She hasn't been to this place since the thugs took over."

Denise decided to continue over to where Corey was. The elderly woman she'd seen coming through the gate got there before she did. Denise then noticed a young man helping the woman bend over to place a flower in front of a picture of Curtis, which sat on the ground surrounded by candles. Denise drew closer and was shocked to realize that the young man and elderly woman she'd observed were her husband and mother. She rushed over to see why she'd come to the park today. Her mother never mentioned that she knew Curtis and she wasn't the type to come to memorial services to pay homage, even if she did know the person.

"Hi, Momma," Denise said. "What brings you all the way out here? You know the doctor ordered you to stay off of your ankle until the swelling goes down."

"Slow down and give your mother a chance to answer your questions, D," her mother replied as she hugged her daughter. She then eased herself onto a nearby bench. "First of all, hello to you, too, D. Second, I helped deliver the young man that was murdered here. And third, since when have you ever known me to take orders from anyone? Now, did I answer all of your questions, honey?" she asked as she grabbed Denise's hand.

"You're so stubborn, Momma. And stop smiling at me. That only works with the men."

"Oh, believe me, angel, it works on everyone, including you. Enough of you, Denise. Corey, how've you been?"

"I'm okay, Momma Di. How about yourself?"

"Hanging in there, Corey," she answered before staring at the sky and saying, "God is good, Corey. Always remember that. I don't care what you call Him, he's merciful to us and he loves us. Everything happens for a reason, Corey, everything. We may not understand what God has planned, but it's not our job to. Just be good to each other, righteous, and let God do his job. This was a sweet young man that the Lord took. Used to hold the door for me whenever I went to buy my Zinfandel. You know they say it helps prevent cancer." She paused and smiled at Corey. "Anyway, your friend would help me to my car but would never take any money from me. Had all the other young fellows scared to death to ask me for change. Told them this was Momma Di's town and not to ask me for anything. I want you two to keep in mind that tomorrow isn't promised to any of us and always remember the good that people did when they were here, not the bad."

"We will, Momma," Corey and Denise replied.

"Hi, Pumpkin. Why are your eyes so red?" Diana asked as she leaned over to kiss Katrina's forehead.

"Mommy hit me," she said in a low, sensitive voice.

"And you probably deserved it. You know Grandma is quick to spank your behind, right?"

"Yes."

"Well I would advise you to get your act together before Grandma has to get busy with her cane. What are you doing over here anyway? Go play with your friends."

"Okay, Grandma. I love you," Katrina said before turning to walk off.

"I love you too, Pumpkin, but I still meant what I said."

"Why did you have that little girl over here with these people, Denise?" Diana inquired.

"I didn't, Momma. I was on my way over here to take her from Corey."

"It's your job to stay on her, Denise, not his. Only a mother can raise a woman. And Corey, stop spoiling that child before she gets so out of hand that you can't control her. Like that young girl...what's her name?"

"Michelle, Momma," Denise replied, embarrassed that she was being chastised in front of everyone.

"Yeah, her...poor girl. I watched her grow up, too. She was like Pumpkin when she was small. But after her momma died, there was no structure in her home. Now look at her, partying half the night, sleeping half the day, and only holding down a part-time job. Corey, you'd better put your foot down before that girl brings you a world of trouble, you hear?"

"I know she plays me like a sucker sometimes,

Momma Di. I'll try to be a little more firm from now on," Corey said, beginning to feel like Denise.

No one paid any attention to the conversation these three were engaged in. Momma Di was swift to tell you about yourself, no matter who you were. Everyone at the park observed her entering it and just waited to see where she was going to sit so they could kindly move somewhere else. It wasn't that they feared her or didn't like her, they just knew how she was and wasn't in the mood to be told off for what they'd been doing wrong.

"Oh, speak of the devil, there's that young girl now," Diana said as she turned her head, hoping Michelle wouldn't catch sight of her.

"Hey, Momma Di!" Michelle yelled from across the playground as she began to run toward her.

"Jesus, it's time to go."

"Be nice, Momma," Denise retorted. "You know how much Michelle loves you."

"I know, I know. I'll behave."

"Hi, sugar," Diana said in a counterfeit manner as Michelle hugged her. "Lord, you smell like a brewery child."

"I'm sorry, Momma Di. I'm in mourning."

"You're supposed to be sad when mourning, not drunk. Who started this 'get drunk and poor liquor for my dead homies' thing anyway? When I was younger, we..."

"Momma."

"What, Denise? I'm sorry, I must be getting too old to be around you and your friends," Diana said, praying that this would excuse her from this now uncomfortable situation.

"Don't even go there, Momma Di. You know you're just as young as the rest of us. Your age is what's in here,"

Michelle said, pointing to her chest.

"I know, child. Anyways, I have to get ready to do my shopping and laundry today, so I'd better get going."

"Momma, it's so nice today. Why don't you spend it with me, Corey, and the kids?" Denise pleaded.

"I can't, baby. This is the only chance I'll get to take care of my business. You know tomorrow's the Lord's Day, and I plan to rest just as He did. Until the evening that is, when your family comes by for dinner."

"Dinner! Can I come, Momma Di, please?" Michelle interceded.

"Well…"

"Oh, let her come by, Momma. You're always talking about receiving blessings for feeding people," Denise stated. "I want to invite Tina, also. You know she passed the bar exam."

"Well, bless her heart. I always knew *she'd* become something," Diana said, staring at Michelle. "Alright, child, Michelle and Tina can come by for dinner, but NOT that darn Jackie. I can't afford to feed all them babies right now. Maybe I'll invite them over one day by themselves. Lord knows somebody needs to help her feed them kids."

"Thanks, Momma," Denise said as she kissed her mother's cheek.

"Corey, help Momma Di up, baby. My ankle's killing me. I think it's going to rain tomorrow," Diana said as she reached out to grab his arm.

"I got you, Momma Di," he replied.

"I hope so, 'cause if I fall, you comin' with me, honey. Where's my grandson? I sat here all this time and just noticed he ain't around."

"Tina's keeping an eye on him for me over by the

swings. Do you want me to bring him over here so you can see him?"

"That's okay, Denise. Just bring him by the house tomorrow."

"Okay. By the way, Momma, nice hat."

"Thank you, baby. You know Momma Di's gotta have her hats. It's my trademark, dear," Diana said as she began walking toward the park's main entrance.

"Corey, are you ready to leave yet?" Denise asked as she threw her arms over his shoulders.

"I guess so. This is becoming a bit depressing. Get the kids and meet me at the gate."

"Alright, I'll just be a second."

"Don't even try it. We both know what you mean by, 'I'll just be a second'. Don't start running your mouth with your girlfriends."

"I won't. I promise," she said before delivering a quick peck to Corey's lips.

"And tell them I said what's up," Corey added as Denise walked away.

"Well, it took you long enough," Tina mumbled to Denise as she rocked Kareem's stroller back and forth. "Got me over here babysitting while you enjoy yourself."

"I'm sorry, girl. I was speaking to my mother. She wants you to come to dinner tomorrow night. Can you make it?"

"Momma Di's cooking? I wouldn't miss it for the world, sis. How *is* your mother? I haven't seen her in years."

"She's fine. She has to have surgery on her ankle. The doctor said it's retaining water and needs to be drained."

"I'm sorry to hear that. I need to call her more often.

You know, I never thanked her for taking care of me after my mother passed. She always said my mother was like a sister to her. She also said you could use a big sister, so it all worked out perfectly."

"You know I despised you when you first moved in, right?"

"Why? I never did anything to you." A look of astonishment fell over Tina's face.

"Because I was used to being the only child. Next thing I know, some pathetic looking teenager was living with me and bossing me around. Plus, you thought you were cute," Denise replied, trying to hold back her grin.

"What! I don't believe you just said that. Shit, I *was* cute," Tina said, flinging her hair back and fluttering her eyes.

"Girl, please, now I *know* that it's time to go. Katrina, c'mon!" Denise shouted and then glanced back to Tina. "You know I love you, sis."

"I love you, too, Denise. I'll see you at your mom's tomorrow."

As Katrina approached her mother, Denise noticed how soiled she'd become and began experiencing the hot sensation that occurs behind your ears right before you explode.

"Katrina, look at you! What did I tell you about being so rough? You act like a boy sometimes."

"She's okay, Denise," Michelle said as she assisted her in wiping the dirt from Katrina's mouth.

"Why is it okay, Michelle? Because she acts like you?"

"Don't get mad at me. I'm not her mother, you are."

"That's right, *I am.* So let me handle this, please."

"Whatever, Denise. I'm outta here." Michelle lifted her beer, took a swig, and began making her way toward the bleachers.

"You know she can't help herself, Denise," Jackie rebuked. "She had it rough growing up. As rugged as she may act, she still wants to be feminine. She just doesn't know how to. I think you really hurt her feelings just now. She looks at your children like a niece and nephew, just as Tina and I look at them. We all look after each other, Denise, but right now, you're wrong."

"And I suppose it's all right when she calls us bitches and tells us to shut the fuck up, right?" Tina interjected.

"That's not what I'm saying. That's her personality, not ours. But it's our responsibility as friends to try and correct her behavior. The same way you two stay on my back about having so many children so early in life without getting an education first."

"You're right, Jackie," Denise said, knowing she was wrong. "She's like a sister to me. I just wish she'd get herself together."

"Then help her. Don't hurt her."

"I'll talk to her tomorrow night."

"What's going on tomorrow night?"

Denise paused and remembered Jackie wasn't invited to dinner. "Um... nothing. I meant to say I'll talk to her tomorrow."

"Oh, okay. Guess I'll see you later, Denise."

"Take care, Jackie. See you later, Tina."

"Yeah, it's about time for me to get going, also. I have a tough case I've been working on. I have to be in court all day Monday, so I'd better get busy."

"Alright, call me later. Maybe we can hook up,"

Denise called out over her shoulder.

As Denise neared the entrance, she noticed Corey standing with his arms folded, tapping his foot and staring at his watch.

"Be back in a second, huh?"

"Oh, be quiet, Corey. I wasn't that long."

"Boy, I swear, when you get around your girlfriends, the verbal Olympics commence. Who won this time? I'm willing to bet that you took the gold again."

"Please, Corey, I'll never have as many medals as you. Let's go." She hit him on the arm and continued past him.

Dusk arrived and Denise put the children to bed. She'd hoped that Tina would have called by now with some exciting plans for the evening, but the phone hadn't rung all night. So, she decided to clean the dishes that'd been left in the sink since breakfast.

Meanwhile, Corey sat in the living room listening to some of his oldies. They reminded him of his parents, well, when they were together anyway. The music would take him back to his early childhood and remind him of how happy his family was at one point. He wanted to have that same happiness with his own family.

"Honey, do you feel like sitting on the front porch with me? I mean, if we're going to end up like the Douglas's one day, we may as well get our practice in now," Denise asked as she stood in the living room's doorway.

"Yeah, why not," he responded while reaching to turn off the stereo. "But I don't see why you think you need practice. You already act like Mrs. Douglas."

"Whatever, Corey, just come on."

"It's really beautiful out here tonight," Corey stated

as he sat on the stairs beside his wife. "And you're really beautiful tonight, D."

"You say that as if I'm not beautiful every night," she replied with her bottom lip protruding as if he'd hurt her feelings.

"You know what I mean, girl."

"Corey, is something bothering you? I mean, besides Curtis' incident."

"I'm just tired, baby. Tired of this city, tired of not finding a decent job, and tired of not providing a better life for you and the kids. Sometimes I feel like grabbing a forty of something and just curling up into a corner with it. You know I've done my share of dirt in these streets, and lately, they've been calling me. You try to do the right thing and sometimes it seems as if it's all in vain."

"Corey, stop it! You're better than that. Sometimes you have to do like my mother said. Just let go, and let God."

"I know, D, I know. I'm just frustrated right now and not thinking straight."

"Things will change, Corey. You'll see. I love you and I've got your back. Do you have anything set up for Monday?"

"Yeah, I have an interview at that new warehouse downtown. I hear they have a pretty decent starting salary and good benefits. I'll just keep my fingers crossed."

"There you go, baby. Think positive. These streets will not benefit you one bit and you know it. This is all a test from God to see what decisions you're going to make. Just remember, whatever you do now will have an impact on you in the future. So keep that in mind before you make your bed, because you'll be the one to lie in it."

"Look at you, baby. This is one of the many reasons that I love you so much. You're so good to me and you're an excellent mother to our children. When I get on my feet, I'm gonna take you out and spoil you until you beg me to stop," he said while struggling to hold back his tears.

"It's nothing, honey. Did you forget 'for rich or for poor, in sickness and in health, 'til death do us part'?"

"I think I may have, but I won't anymore. Thanks, D. And thank you, Lord, for letting that heat wave finally move on."

# CHAPTER
# 7

# Katrina:
# 9-8-86

"*K*atrina! Give the crayon back to him. He had it first. Now, this is the third time that I've had to speak to you today, honey. Do you want me to call your mother?"

"No, Mrs...." Katrina paused and looked at the classroom's ceiling as if waiting for her teacher's name to fall from it.

"Green, sweetheart. My name is Mrs. Green."

"No, Mrs. Green," Katrina answered.

It was the first day of school. The first day of an extensive education that Denise and Corey spent many months preparing for. For Katrina, this was the first day of freedom. The first day of spending time with a group of people who were unfamiliar to her. Actually, this was the first day for her to get her groove on. This White woman, who'd just asked if she should call her mother, posed no threat. Earlier that day, Denise explained to her daughter she had to work and wouldn't be able to stay with her on the first day of school.

What she didn't know was Katrina didn't want her there in the first place. Today had been well anticipated by Katrina. Just the idea of her mother not being present was enough to fuel the flickering flame of mischief she concealed for far too long. If Mrs. Green would have known how irrelevant her threats were, she wouldn't have bothered making them.

"Okay, children, I want you to put your things away and meet me in the reading corner."

Mrs. Green was an elderly woman who'd spent half her life in the educational field. She taught everything from entry-level college courses to middle-high school and elementary classes. She finally found herself teaching kindergarten and thought, at her age, this was where she wanted to retire. Sometimes she wished she still worked with a more mature group of people. She'd worked with urban children most of her career and felt as if this was where she belonged. She would often tell her colleagues she had an understanding of most inner-city youth and bragged how students would come to her for advice whenever their lives were in chaos. What she didn't know was children like Katrina were a new species unknown to man, and there were no books to read, nor seminars to attend, which would inform teachers on how to deal with them.

She was very attractive for her age. She always wore a bun on the back of her head and an antique, wooden barrette held her partially gray hair in place. She had a pair of reading glasses that never left her face, even when she wasn't reading. The glasses had a silver colored chain connected to each of its arms, and everyone was amazed at how the spectacles balanced themselves on the tip of her abnormally long nose. The way her green eyes stared at you whenever she became infuriated assisted her in getting her point across whenever she deployed her disciplinary tactics.

"Katrina, will you be joining us?"

"Yes," she replied.

"When Katrina?"

"As soon as I finish this picture for my mommy, Mrs. Teacher," Katrina said, never lifting her eyes from her masterpiece.

"It's Mrs. Green, Katrina, and I want you to sit with us now. We will all have time to finish our pictures later," she said while being mindful not to let Katrina know her anger was slowly reaching its boiling point.

"Okay, Mrs. Jean," Katrina replied with a smirk. Katrina was very intelligent, and although she did remember her teacher's name, she didn't feel this stranger, whom she just met, deserved any respect from her. She also found it much more amusing toying with her and watching her pale face change colors.

"Mrs. Green, dear, Mrs. Green," she growled though gritted teeth.

Katrina was now five going on twenty-five and although her mother had her under control, Katrina felt as if she had the rest of the world right where she wanted them. And she did, including Corey. Katrina was the personification of 'Oh, she's so cute.' You know the type: big bright eyes, bubbly smile, dimples, the whole nine yards. It normally takes a few years before a child becomes conceited, but somehow this child contracted the illness much earlier. Instead of using it to get want she wanted, she used it as, 'I'm too cute for you to get mad at.' So now Mrs. Green had a stuck-up, spoiled tomboy from the hood who she'd just been told would be her responsibility to change into a respectable little girl within the next ten months, and if she couldn't do that, then maybe she was in the wrong profession. And, to top it off, she would have to endure all of this for a few measly grand a year.

There were a few other demanding obstacles Mrs. Green and her colleagues must overcome each day. For example, there's crack baby Tommy who can't sit still for more than five minutes at a time. Then there's Rita, whose mother brings home a different man every night so now her child has mysteriously picked up the habit of fondling every boy in the classroom. Oh, and let us not forget little Laurence, a.k.a. Big L, whose father is serving a life sentence for killing two men during an armed robbery. For some reason, this little fellow can't seem to cease in extorting everything his classmates possess.

None of this mattered, however. Mrs. Green's job was to spend seven hours a day teaching these wonderful children how to behave, by any means necessary. She was in this war alone. Her fellow troops, or 'parents', had retreated. She was faced with having to win the battle herself, and her enemies were multiplying at an enormous rate: drugs, rap music, alcohol, fat gold chains, guns, deadbeat dads, shit— deadbeat moms, and absentee parents, even though they're home with their children. And then there were the infamous family youth services whose only concern was to make sure urban children would be so screwed up when they became adults, they'd feel more comfortable receiving three "hots-and-a-cot" in someone's correctional facility than to face the world as a free human being. Mrs. Green, like many other dedicated soldiers, realized it was a war and vowed to prevail until their retirement or death, whichever comes first.

"Okay, children, I would like for you to return to your desks so that we may prepare for lunch."

"What's for lunch, Mrs. Green," a raspy voice shouted

from the back of the class.

"We're having turkey and cheese sandwiches, Laurence. Make sure you put your book back on the shelf neatly."

"And what's for snack?"

"We have apples."

"Good! I like apples, Mrs. Green," he told her as he licked his lips.

"I like apples, too, Mrs. Dean," Katrina said, hoping to get her teacher's attention.

At this point, Mrs. Green's tolerance for Katrina's misuse of her name had become too much for her to handle. She decided to ignore the fact Katrina insisted to continue to call her by different names, and chose to just answer her as if she'd done nothing wrong. Maybe eventually this would change her behavior.

"That's nice, Katrina. I really like apples, too," she replied.

Katrina could sense the lack of interest in her teacher's voice. She began to notice her teacher was no longer annoyed with her plan to continuously embarrass her in front of the other students, and was not going to patronize her anymore by continuing to participate in her juvenile conversations.

Lunch was served and Katrina suddenly found herself being the victim of the same crime she committed a few times herself.

"Give me your apple," Laurence said as he snatched it from Katrina's hand.

Now, Big L *was* actually much bigger and stronger than the rest of the children and would have probably gotten away with this with any other child. However, this wasn't any other child. He quickly shoved the apple into his pocket, expecting Katrina to begin screaming like most children, but not today.

"Ow!! Mrs. Green, my lip, my lip!"

"Oh my God, Laurence, you're bleeding! What happened?" she asked as she placed a napkin over his mouth.

"She punched me. She punched me hard!"

"Who punched you?"

"Gatina did it."

"Why, Katrina? Why do you insist on doing what you want to do? Both of you follow me to the nurse's office. And as for you, *Miss Katrina*, I'm calling your mother. I have had it up to here with you," she said as she raised her hand and placed it in front of her forehead.

"But…"

"No buts! Let's go!"


"But Mommy, he *did* take the apple from me," Katrina said as she held her hands over her face, attempting to conceal how hard she was crying.

"Whatever, girl! I've spoken to you all of your life about taking things that don't belong to you! You won't be satisfied until they put you in a home for bad girls! You'll be the only five-year-old in the whole building! Go to your room and change your clothes! I don't want to see you until it's time for dinner! Do you understand me?"

"Yes, Mommy," she answered through her tears.

As Katrina ran upstairs, Corey entered the house just in time to see Katrina's back turn the corner at the top of the stairs and head towards her bedroom.

"D, what the hell is going on? I could hear you yelling halfway down the block."

"Katrina is what's going on, Corey. I'm tired of talking to her about the same shit. Every time she interacts with other children, there's a problem. This time I get a phone call at work, DURING A MEETING no less, saying that she took some innocent little boy's apple and then punched the kid in the mouth!"

"Damn!!" Corey said with a slight grin on his face.

"Damn what, Corey? You look as if you're enjoying this little fiasco of hers."

"It's not that, D. I'm just glad to hear that my baby can handle herself." Corey's grin was now becoming a chuckle.

"What! Corey, I don't..."

"I'm just kidding, D" he said as he embraced her and kissed her on the cheek. "I'll go upstairs and talk to her."

"Oh no the hell you won't, Mr. Softy. I'm gonna deal with her later after she takes a nap and does some repenting for her actions today."

"Fine, it's your child. She's only mine when she's behaving herself," he jokingly mumbled as he began to open the refrigerator.

"I heard that, smart-ass. What are you so chipper about anyway?"

"Nothing, except for you'd better watch the way you speak to a working man."

"Oh my God, Corey, you got the job! I told you things would begin to look up for you as long as you were patient," she said with tears in her eyes as she reached out to hug and kiss him.

"Thank you, D. And I want to apologize to you for thinking so negatively before," he said as he continued to hold her. "You know that I would never do anything to jeopardize you or our children. I just want the best for you guys."

"I know, Corey, but how about jeopardizing yourself?"

"Yeah, I know…that, too."

"Wow, don't try to sound so sincere next time."

"I'm sorry, D, but you know that I don't give a fuck about nothing but you and my babies."

"Yeah, but all that me and your babies care about is you. Are you hungry?"

"I don't know…maybe a little."

"A little? I guess that's why you've been standing there all this time with the fridge open?"

"No, I think that's just a habit we men have. I think we hope it will miraculously fill up right before our eyes. You know, with some chips, a couple of hoagies, or a case of beer or something."

"Beer? You haven't had a drink in years."

"I know, but I think I'm going to have a celebration drink later with some of my boys."

"Alright, Corey, remember what happened the last time you went out for a celebration drink with your so-called *boys*. I think it was at your little bachelor party. They painted your fingernails, put lipstick on you, and left you laying pissy drunk in the prostitute area with your pants and underwear halfway to your knees. They even took pictures of you and posted them around the neighborhood with the words 'Another Innocent Rape Victim' written on the bottom."

"Yeah, I remember. I guess you'll never let me live that one down, huh?"

"Nope. Shoot, the whole damn town still remembers. That's probably why your ass couldn't find a job," Denise shouted right before bursting into a rage of laughter.

"Whoa, you're on a roll today, aren't you? How much

are they paying you for this act?" he asked, trying very hard not to laugh about the incident himself.

"Not as much as they paid you for your act, I'll bet." Her laughter became uncontrollable at this point and she began to cough.

"Good for your ass. I hope you choke," he said as he began to laugh with her.

"Oh, don't get mad at me because you're a rape victim, bud…" she said before falling to the floor and grabbing her stomach. The tears were now pouring from her eyes.

"Look at how silly you are, Denise. You can't even finish your damn jokes. I'm going to meet Roman. I'll be back later," he said as he stepped over her and headed for the door.

"Be careful, honey!" she shouted as he closed the door. "Just yell rape if they can't take no for an answer."

Corey could still hear his wife laughing three houses away from his. What was even stranger was that he couldn't seem to stop laughing himself.

"Damn, Denise. God I love that woman," he said while shaking his head and walking towards Roman's house.

# CHAPTER
# 8

"Mommy, can I get up now?" Katrina yelled from the top of the stairs, too fearful of asking her mother face to face.

"Yes, you can come downstairs, Pumpkin. I was just on my way up to wake you. It's time for dinner."

Katrina entered the kitchen rubbing her eyes, attempting to focus on the food that sat on the table.

"Hi, Pumpkin," Denise said as she bent over and kissed Katrina. "How was your nap? Do you feel better?"

"Yes, Mommy. Where's Daddy?"

"He should be picking up Kareem by now. I'm surprised that he didn't call."

"Maybe he didn't call because you had a fight after you told me to go upstairs?"

"We weren't fighting."

"But I heard you yelling at him, telling him not to drink and wear lipstick with his pants down anymore, and you sounded like you were crying."

"Oh, we were laughing and joking about something that happened a long time ago. We weren't fighting."

"What happened, Mommy?"

"Nothing, Pumpkin. Maybe I'll tell you when you get older. Now sit down and eat your food. We need to talk."

"Okay."

"Now tell me, why do you feel like you have to always take things from other kids without asking?"

"Mommy, I'm not lying about my apple today. I watched him take crayons, toys, and books from kids all day, and I told myself that as soon as he tried that with me, I was gonna punch him right in the face. So when he did, that's what I did."

"I understand that, Katrina, but I've watched you take things from other children and hit them many times before today's incident. So I don't know if you're telling the truth or not. Now, I want you to promise me I won't hear another story about you stealing from kids or bullying them for their belongings. Is that understood?"

"Yes, Mommy, but it was *my* apple," Katrina stated in a stern voice.

"I believe you, but the next time you have this problem, tell your teacher about it. Okay?"

"She doesn't like me, Mommy," Katrina said just before remembering *why* her teacher didn't like her. Suddenly, she began to feel as if she'd just opened another can of worms.

"Why would you say that, honey?"

"Um, never mind, Mommy. I don't want to talk about school anymore today," she said while holding her head down and giving her mother the impression that she just had one of the worst days of her life. She hoped maybe this would cause her mother to show some compassion and forget about the statement she just uttered about her teacher.

"Are you sure, Pumpkin?"

"Yes, I'm sure."

"My goodness, where is your father? It's almost eight o'clock and he still hasn't gotten…"

Before Denise could finish her sentence, she heard

someone tapping at the front door. "Don't tell me he forgot his keys again," Denise mumbled before opening the door.

"Hey, Mrs. D. I decided to bring Kareem home since it was starting to get late. His father never showed up."

"What! I am so sorry, Brenda. He left a couple of hours ago to meet that darn Roman and I thought he would pick the baby up before coming home," Denise said in an apologetic, yet furious tone.

"Oh, come on, Mrs. D, it's no big deal. You know I live right around the corner. Plus, I'll just charge you overtime for it at the end of the week...just kidding."

"Thank you so much, Brenda. Would you like to come in for a minute?"

"Sure, Mrs. D, I wanna see my little friend anyway. Where is she?"

"She's in the living room watching television. Go on and have a seat."

"Thanks, Mrs. D. Hey boy! Wow, Mrs. D, I didn't know that you still had this little mutt running around here."

"I heard you, Miss Brenda!" Katrina yelled from the living room. "He's not a mutt. He's a shawawa!!"

"Oh, *excuse me*, Miss Thang," Brenda said as she entered the room where Katrina was. "I meant to say shawawa."

"Pumpkin, who told you that your dog was a Chihuahua?" Denise asked, astonished that her daughter even knew what a Chihuahua was.

"I can tell because he's very small. I saw one on television before. He just needs a haircut really badly."

"Katrina, a Chihuahua doesn't have long hair. We don't know what kind of dog this is. Most likely, he's mixed with something and that's why Miss Brenda called him a mutt."

"I'm sorry, Mrs. Denise, but there are Chihuahua's with long hair. I read about them in school. You know I've been thinking about becoming a vet someday."

"Mommy, how do dogs become mixed?" Katrina interrupted.

"Well, when different breeds mate..." Denise paused after realizing where the conversation was headed. "Just watch television with Miss Brenda, Pumpkin. You have company now, so we'll talk about dogs later, okay?" As Denise quickly made her way out of the living room, she thought to herself, *'God I hope that worked.'*

"So, Katrina, how have you been? How's school?" Brenda asked as she sat on the sofa beside her.

"I'm alright, but I hate school. I got in trouble on the first day."

"What happened?"

"I punched a boy in the mouth and made him bleed."

"Wow. What made you do that?" Brenda said, not the least bit surprised with Katrina's statement.

"He stole my apple from me, so I hit him."

"Well, what are you going to do the next time that happens?"

"Tell my teacher."

"Good. Then you learned a lesson."

Brenda was a fifteen-year-old high school student who lived around the corner from Katrina. She came from a long line of the neighborhood baby-sitting industry. Momma Di was nanny to her mother who, years later, watched over Denise when she was younger. Denise was about eight or nine when Brenda was born and looked after Brenda as she grew up. Although Denise and Brenda weren't too far apart in age, it had always been custom to refer to your elders as *Auntie* or *Uncle*, out of respect. When Denise returned home after college, Brenda picked up the habit of calling her Mrs. D rather than of Auntie D. It wasn't common for someone from this neighborhood to leave for college and return with a degree in anything. Many teens attempted to pursue a higher education, but most of them returned shortly after, partying themselves into a coma after the first year. Brenda held Denise in high esteem after she'd successfully returned home with a degree, and thought that calling her *Mrs.* showed more honor than Auntie.

Brenda admired Denise and had all intentions of following in her footsteps, with the exception of getting pregnant in college, of course. She maintained a 4.0 grade point average and kept herself busy by being involved in everything from glee and chess clubs to debate teams and student council. She never got in any trouble in the neighborhood. Most of her peers looked at her as a nerd and pretty much left her alone. Brenda hoped that one day Katrina would look to her as a mentor just as she looked at Katrina's mother.

"So, Katrina, I know you're kinda young, but do you ever think about what you want to be when you grow up?"

"Yup," she replied.

"Well?"

"I want to be famous," Katrina answered, never taking her eyes from the television.

"There's many ways to become famous, Katrina. How do you plan on doing it?"

Katrina sat motionless for a minute before responding.

"I don't know. I just want everybody around here to know me."

"But a lot of people around here already know you. Don't you want everyone in the world to know you?"

"Not really. Everybody knows my Mommy and Daddy around here, but I want them to know me, too," she said as she turned to face Brenda. "What about you?"

"I think I want to be a vet, but I've been focusing on becoming a social worker."

"What's that doing?"

"That's someone who works in the community and tries to help families with problems. But I really just want to work with kids."

"Will that make you famous?" Katrina asked with her left eyebrow slightly raised.

"Yes, in the neighborhood, I guess."

Katrina turned toward the television and attempted to catch a glimpse of one of her favorite commercials. She began to sing the commercial's jingle. When it was over, she turned to face Brenda again, this time with her legs folded Indian style, and placed both of her hands under her chin. Brenda sensed Katrina was pondering something, but couldn't figure whether it was going to be a question or an answer.

"Well, Auntie Brenda, I guess I want to be a social worker, too," she said with a smile on her face.

"Wow, Pumpkin, I'm really proud of you," she said as she reached out to embrace her.

"Denise! D!!" Corey yelled as he leaned on the door to the hallway closet.

"What, Corey?" Denise answered as she began running toward the front door. "What happened?"

"Uh, nothing. Can you help me to the bathroom? I can't see."

"Oh my God, Corey, YOU'RE DRUNK!!" she said

with a look of absolute repugnance on her face.

"No, I'm not," he slurred. "I just can't see."

"Maybe if you took off these damn sunglasses, you'd be able to *see*," she whispered as she reached to take them from his face. "I don't believe you're allowing Katrina and Brenda to see you in this condition."

"Oh…hi, Pumpkin. You know Daddy loves you. Yes him do, baby," he said as he stumbled toward the living room. "Heeyy, Brennndaaa!"

"No, Corey," Denise demanded as she grabbed his arm and attempted to escort him upstairs.

"No? Why no, huh? You know how much I love her. Why it always got to be no? You don't love me no more, do you, Denise? Huh?" Tears began to swell in his eyes. "Nobody loves me. And I loves ebbrybody. Don't I, Denise?"

"Yes, Corey, you love everybody," she whispered in disgust with her teeth clenched as she dragged him up the stairs.

"I don't think I feel too well, Denise. My stomach hurts. I think I gotta…"

"COREY!!!"

# CHAPTER 9

# Kareem:
# 10-8-93

"*H*urry up, Kareem. You're always the last one to leave the building," Katrina impatiently yelled with her arms folded as she stood at the entrance to the school's playground.

"I'm coming, Pumpkin. Why you always gotta yell at me?" Kareem replied as he simultaneously tried to adjust his book bag, fix his glasses, and run toward his sister.

"Because you're always so unorganized. Look at you! Papers falling from your bag, shoelaces untied. You're a mess."

"Pumpkin, look, I got all A's on my report card."

"So what, you're still a mess."

Kareem began to sing, "Don't hate, don't hate, don't hate, don't hate, don't hate. You're just mad because you don't get good grades."

"Shut up before I smack you." Katrina stopped walking, faced Kareem, and raised her hand towards him.

"If you do, I'm telling Mommy."

"Whatever, you little bitch."

"Ooo... I'm telling Mommy you cursed again."

"Yeah, and what is she gonna do?  Beat me ag..."

"Yo, what up, Pumpkin," Laurence interrupted.

"Hey, what's up, L?"

"Which way y'all walking?" he asked.

"Probably through the park," she replied.  "I want to see if anybody's hangin' out there before we go home."

"Pumpkin, Mommy told us to come straight home after school and you know what she said about going to that park."

"Will you shut the hell up!" she shouted.  "I *know* what Mommy said...it's dangerous.  But, guess what?  I'm dangerous, too."

"Maybe you should listen to your brother," Laurence interceded.  "It is a little crazy at that park now.  It ain't like when we were little.  The high schoolers are out of control. Everybody's in a gang now, so somebody's always getting shot down there."

"Big L, I know you ain't punkin' out on me. Everybody at that park knows us.  Plus, we'll be high schoolers next year, so we might as well start hanging with them now.  We're a team, L, and you know I got your back."

Katrina and Laurence remained friends after kindergarten. Their story was similar to her parents' story in that she'd socked Laurence when they first met, just as her mother struck Corey upon their first encounter. The only difference was these two had absolutely no aspirations of becoming an item.  There *was* one leisure activity they did enjoy though: fighting. Katrina had become well-known for it and was excellent at it. Girls her age were afraid of her and those who were older than she was, were glad they were.  It meant not having to deal with her. Laurence, or Big L as he liked to be called, became her running mate during the last seven years. Although he was only thirteen, he was almost six feet tall and every bit of two hundred twenty-five plus pounds. They weren't bullies but, just as Katrina always wanted, she was "famous" in her neighborhood.

"Shouldn't we at least drop your brother off first?" Laurence insisted.

"Yeah, you're right. C'mon, bubblehead," she said to Kareem as she gently nudged the back of his head.

"Stop, Pumpkin!" he replied.

"How was school today, guys?" Denise asked as she sat in her lazy boy and rubbed her stomach.

"It was great, Mommy," Kareem replied. "Mommy?"

"Yes, baby."

"Katrina cursed at me again!" he said as he pointed his finger at her.

"Katrina, what did I tell you about your mouth?"

"He was aggravating me."

"Yeah, well now you're aggravating me! Go to your room. Your father will deal with you later."

"Mom, I was about to go to the park with my friends."

"What the hell did you just say to me, girl? I said go to your room. I don't care what you were *about* to do, and you'll be dealt with when your father gets home."

"Yeah, *if* he comes home," Katrina mumbled as she began to stomp upstairs.

"I would advise you to watch your mouth, Miss," Denise shouted.

"Mommy, look at my report card."

"Let's see what you've got there, Kareem. Wow! Good job, baby. I am so proud of you. You've been doing an excellent job in school. I don't know what your sister's problem is. I don't understand why she can't be more like you and less like the rest of the garbage she chooses to hang with."

"I don't know either, Mommy. Hey, Mommy?"

"Yes, honey."

"When are you going to have your baby?"

"The doctor says in about two months. Sometimes I think you're more excited than I am."

"I am. Is it a boy or a girl?"

"I don't know. What do you want, a little brother or a little sister?"

"It doesn't matter. Sometimes I want a sister and hope she'll treat me better than Katrina does, but it really doesn't matter. I just want you to hurry up so that you'll be skinny again like you used to be."

"What's that supposed to mean? Are you calling me fat?"

"No, Mommy, you're just really big."

Kareem's comments were not meant to intentionally hurt his mother. Kids, unlike adults, usually say whatever comes to their minds without regard of the impact the words may have on those they are speaking to.

Kareem was, without a doubt, his mother's child. He took school very serious and had great respect for his mother. His relationship with his father was not great but could have been much better. Corey spent more time at work and with his friends than he did with his family, and this had a huge impact on their 'father-son relationship'. Kareem was 'Momma's little boy'. Katrina knew this and despised him for it.

Kareem was a very handsome and intriguing boy. He had his father's looks and charisma but his mother's intellect and ambition to become something. Some kids would taunt him and call him a 'pretty boy'. This usually came to an end whenever his sister found out about it. See, it was acceptable for *her* to ridicule and detest him, because he was still her blood. There were days where she would beat him up first thing in the morning, then turn around and beat someone else up that afternoon for attempting to make fun of him. He *was* a 'pretty boy' so to speak. His skin was incredibly dark, yet smooth and unblemished. He had hair like his mother: jet black, very silky, and curly in appearance. Sometimes he wished he could get into a fight and have his face badly scarred, hoping he wouldn't be teased so much if it was. The fact that Katrina was his sister and Big L was her best friend eradicated any chances of that ever happening.

"Hi, Daddy"

"Hey, Kareem. Hey, D."

"Wow, you're home early," Denise replied nonchalantly. "No *overtime,* as you always say?"

"Don't start, D. I'm tired."

"Yeah well, I'm tired, too. Tired of you not being here, tired of us not conversing. Tired of what's happening to us."

"Denise, must we do this in front of Kareem?"

"No, you're right, Corey. We'll talk later."

"I'm going out with Roman later."

"If you do, I won't be here when you come home. Just remember that."

"Here we go again. Whatever, Denise, do what you want." Although those were the words that came from his mouth, Corey *did* take heed to what his wife said and had no intentions of leaving the house that evening.

"Mommy, why do you and Daddy argue so much?"

"This isn't an argument, Kareem. It's a misunderstanding. I just had to set some things straight with your father…you know, put him in his place," she responded as she winked at Corey with a smile.

"Okay, Denise, don't you confuse that boy as to who wears the pants around here."

"No problem, honey, as long as you're not confused to the fact that if I didn't wash those pants, you'd be ass out, literally," she smugly replied.

"Oh, here come the jokes again. I'm going upstairs to take a nap."

"Sweet dreams, baby," she sarcastically yelled.

"Mommy, can I go outside and play for a little while?"

"Sure. Do you have any homework?"

"Nope, it's Friday."

"Okay, you know the rule…"

"Yeah, yeah, *have your behind in here when those street lights come on,*" they sang in unison.

"Mommy, can I have a snack?" Katrina asked as she entered the kitchen.

"No, but you can sit your smart ass at this table so we can talk."

"Never mind, I'll just go upstairs and wait for dinner."

"Katrina, SIT!! Don't make me rush you, girl. I mean it!"

"Alright Momma, I'm sitting," Katrina replied, but

not before sucking her teeth and rolling her eyes.

"That's exactly what I'm talking about Katrina. What is your problem? Why do you insist on defying me so much? Your brother…"

"That's the problem, Mom. My brother, my 'wonderful' brother. Mr. 'can't do no wrong'. It seems like ever since he got his first grades last year, you've totally ignored me. Everything is Kareem this and Kareem that. I'm the oldest and you want me to look up to him. Do you have any idea how ridiculous you make me feel?"

"What's all the yelling about, Denise?" Corey asked as he entered the kitchen.

"Katrina and her mouth, Corey. I swear, everyday it's something new. I can't deal with this anymore. I'm pregnant, you're never around, and I have to deal with her on top of everything else. I'm tired, Corey, tired," Denise said as tears began to dispense from her eyes.

"Stop crying, D," he said, wiping the tears from her face. "What's your problem, Miss?"

"Nothing, Daddy."

"Don't 'nothing Daddy' me. This isn't the first time I've gotten news like this about you. Actually, everyone's been telling me stories about you and your little friend Laurence. I've just been too busy to take time to deal with you, but it's coming to an end. Do you understand me, Pumpkin?"

"Yeah."

"YEAH?"

"I mean, yes."

"Go upstairs. I'm giving you a week to think about your behavior."

"A week?"

"Did I stutter? And I think you'd better move your

ass before this civil conversation becomes physical. Do you hear me?"

"Yes, Daddy," she mumbled as she left the kitchen.

"If I hear any stomping, I'm coming up to break both legs so we won't have that problem anymore, either," he yelled as he looked over his shoulder to catch a final glimpse of her.

"You alright, D?"

"No, Corey, I'm not alright."

"What else is wrong?"

"We're wrong, Corey. We don't talk anymore. You're never here. Ever since you had that first 'drink' with Roman a few years ago, our relationship has been steadily going downhill. You work all day and you're at the bar half the night. We had so many plans for our future and I'm watching them drift away. We need prayer, Corey, or this is going to crumble."

"We still have those plans, baby. I..."

"How can we still have those plans, Corey? You've spent enough money on liquor over the past few years to buy a new Mercedes!"

"I realize that I've been squandering a lot of money, and I'm sorry. I was broke for so long, I didn't know how to act when I got my hands on a few dollars. I promise from now on that I'll remember the dreams that we once shared, and I'll try to continue to fulfill them for you."

"For *us*, Corey," she reminded him.

"Yes, for us, D. Is anything else bothering you?"

"I want you to spend time with us like you used to. You know, go out together as a family. I want you to spend more time with the kids, especially Katrina. We're losing her and I don't know how to get her back. Do you remember

Maria?"

"I think so. Her daughter's name is Rita, right? She was in a few of Katrina's classes over the years. Why?"

"Well… Rita's pregnant."

"What! She's only what, like thirteen or fourteen, isn't she?"

"Exactly, that's what I mean. We have a daughter, too."

"But I've never even seen Pumpkin with a boy. Shit, between you and me, sometimes I wonder about her. She's tougher than half the real gangsters around here," he boasted with a smile.

"Corey, there's nothing wrong with our daughter. She acts like you used to. I just wanted to tell you about Rita to stress how imperative it is for us to get our children away from this neighborhood. I'm not saying girls don't get pregnant at a young age in the suburbs, but it's at a much lower rate than here. Katrina is beginning to remind me of Michelle, and I swore I wouldn't allow any of my children to turn out like her."

"Speaking of children, where's Kareem?"

"He's playing outside with his friends."

"Locally, I hope," he said while walking toward the front door to check on him. "Which reminds me, we're moving out of this house. You're right. We do have to get out of this ghetto. I found a nice house right outside of town. The neighborhood is better and it's still close enough for me to commute to my job. The children don't have to change schools and you can still be close to everything, as well."

"When were you going to let me know about all of this? Did it ever occur to you that I may have wanted to incorporate my input into these plans of yours?"

"I was going to surprise you after the baby was born, but I was hoping it might make you feel a little better since you've been so down lately."

"Well when can I see it?" she excitedly asked.

"We can drive out there tomorrow, if you like."

"Yes, I'd love that. But what I'd love even more is if you came over here and gave me a kiss."

Corey walked over to her and embraced her. "I love you, Denise."

"I love you too, Corey. You can go and finish checking on your son now."

Corey opened the front door and momentarily stood motionless as he proudly witnessed his son run from one end of the block to the other with a football under his arm.

"Touchdown!" Kareem yelled as he began his personal celebration dance near the intersection.

"That's it, Kareem! Good job!" Corey shouted as he applauded his son.

"Hi, Daddy," Kareem yelled as he began running toward his front porch. "I miss you. Where've you been?"

"Aw c'mon, Kareem, we're not finished playing yet," one of the other players stated.

"Yeah, Kareem, just because you scored doesn't mean the game is over. C'mon," another added.

"Wait a minute, y'all. I'm coming."

Corey reached down, grabbed his son, and tossed him in the air. "What's up, youngster?" he asked.

"Nothing. Where are you going, Daddy?"

"Nowhere. I just came outside to check on you and count how many touchdowns you make." Corey paused for a moment and remembered the conversation he just had with his wife about spending more time with them. "Actually, I wanted to know if I could be a steady quarterback for you guys."

"Daddy, what do you know about this?" he said as he held the football in his father's face. "You don't want none of this. This is a man's sport," he said as he stuck his chest out and taunted his father.

"Oh yeah, then what are you playing for?" Corey said as he began to tickle his son on the neck. "I used to play football in high school, boy."

"Like you said Daddy, used to. Now you're old."

"Old? I'll show you old." Corey placed Kareem under his arm, posed as if he were a Heisman Trophy, and ran, or slowly jogged, toward the street to join in on the football game.

"Okay, fellas, let's huddle…"

"Come and eat, guys," Denise yelled from her porch.

"Alright, honey. Let's go, Kareem. It's been fun, fellas. Maybe we'll finish this on Sunday. That's the official football day."

"Okay. See you, Mr. Lambert. Peace, Kareem," they shouted.

"See ya'll tomorrow," Kareem replied as he began running toward his house.

"Hey, wait up, son!"

"Nope. Catch up, old man"

"I've got your old man," Corey said as he chased Kareem into the house.

"I know one thing, you two have about three seconds to get up from this table without washing your hands and two of them are already gone."

"Sorry, D."

"Sorry, Mommy. Race you, Daddy."

"That's okay, Kareem. I forfeit. I'm burned out. You can go first."

"That's more like it, guys," she said upon their return. "How was the game?"

"It was great, Mommy. We were winning by two touchdowns when you called us in. I didn't know Daddy could throw a football that well," he said as he stuffed another piece of bread into his mouth.

"Really," Denise said as she gave her husband a look of satisfaction.

"Whoa, slow down, Walter Payton. Your food isn't going anywhere," Corey said while rubbing his son's head.

"Who's Walter Payton, Dad?"

"Who's Walter Payton? He's one of the greatest players to ever touch a football."

"I thought it was Herschel Walker."

"Oh please, son, get a grip. Just because he played for your favorite team doesn't mean he was any good."

"Was so!"

"Was not."

"Corey, you sound worse than he does."

"Yeah, Daddy, can we change the subject to something other than football?" Katrina mumbled.

"No problem. What do you want to talk about, something feminine?" he sarcastically inquired while smiling at his wife.

"I don't think so, Daddy, just anything but football."

"Well, make a suggestion since you're so smart, sis."

"Let's talk about something funny like the corny rap

music you and Mommy used to listen to back in the old days," she snickered.

"Corny rap music? Old days? What are we, ancient?" Corey replied, appalled by the statement his daughter made. "How dare you make a comparison of our music to the trash that you guys listen to today?"

"You tell her, honey," Denise replied as she proudly stuck out her chest.

"Rap music was about talent and skills when we were younger. Then, one day, rich White people saw there was money in it and exploited it to profit from it. Next thing you know, gangster rap was born and things in the hood haven't been the same since. All men became thugs and all women became hoes. Nowadays, it doesn't matter if you have skills or not, as long you can be the dancing jig that they want you to be on stage."

"Dag, Daddy, why does everything have to be a speech when you talk to us? It's just music, you know."

"If that's what you wanna call it, Pumpkin. But your father and I are not going to allow you to ever think all women are hoes and bitches or that the only way for you to make something of yourselves is to sell drugs or rob and kill each other just because some song tells you this is the way we should behave because we're Black and live in the ghetto. Imagine where we could be if everyone sang about getting yourself out of the ghetto. The way rap music influences everyone, the ghetto would be empty."

"Maybe I should've picked something different to talk about," Katrina stated in a depressed tone.

"Yeah, smarty," Kareem added.

"Shut up, Kareem, before I do a 1-8-7 on you!"

"That's enough, Pumpkin. That's exactly what I'm

talking about. A thirteen-year-old girl should not know what a 1-8-7 is."

"Well, that's what they said happened to Curtis back in the day."

"Damn it, girl!! Go upstairs! And the next time I hear you say those numbers, they'd better be part of someone's phone number or social security card! Now go!"

"Sorry, Daddy," Katrina said as she left the kitchen.

"Calm down, Corey. Are you alright?"

"I'm fine, D. I swear that girl is gonna make me choke her."

"Where are you going?"

"To bed," he replied.

"You haven't finished eating your dinner."

"I lost my appetite. Goodnight."

"She always messes up everything, Mommy. Who's Curtis anyway?"

"He was a friend of your father's many years ago but was killed at the park one day. Your father saw the whole thing and it still bothers him."

"Who did it?"

"Someone who's serving many years in prison for it, baby."

"Why did he do it?"

"I guess he felt that he had his reasons. That's why your father is so hard on you guys about your grades, these streets, and your character as African Americans. Just make sure you always do well in school and make plans to get as far away from this place as possible when you graduate, alright? Now, hurry and finish your food so you can take your bath and get ready for bed."

"Okay, Mommy, but it's Friday. Can't I watch TV

before I go to sleep?"

    "After your bath, and only for one hour."

    "Thanks, Mom.  I love you."

    "I love you, too, Kareem.  Katrina, come downstairs and wash these dishes!"

# CHAPTER 10

## Malcom:
## 1-25-94

"C'mon, push, Denise.    Good," the nurse coached.

"Come on child, breathe."

"OH GOD, MOMMA!   I'M BREATHING, I'M BREATHING!!!  Does it look like I'm holding my breath to you?!"

"Calm down, D.  It's almost over, honey."

"Shut the hell up, Corey!  Get out!  Why the hell are you in here anyway?  This is all your faaauuul...!!!"

"Okay, D, I'll be right outside, baby."

"No, no, I'm sorry, Corey.  Please, hold my hand."

"You're doing great, Denise.  I can see the head," the doctor said.  "Now give me one good push and it's over."

"Just cut me open and take it out!!  Give me drugs! Give me something, PLEASE!!"

"Denise, you're breaking my hand!" Corey shrieked.

"Shut up before I break your face.  This is your fault!"

"Here it comes, Denise.  Good, good. That's it. And....

congratulations, dear, you have a beautiful baby boy."

"Oh my God, D, he's beautiful," Corey whispered. "Look, he's already smiling."

"He sure is a beautiful child, son," Diana said. "Lord, look at those eyes. They're light brown just like his grandfather's." Diana placed her hand over the newborn's forehead and quietly began praying over him. "Lord, thank You for blessing these two with such a beautiful child. Please bless this child with all of Your beautiful attributes. Teach him kindness, respect, and wisdom, Lord. Guide this child toward Your Kingdom, Lord, and all that is good. Thank You, Lord. Amen."

"That was a lovely prayer, Momma," Diana sluggishly said as she reached for her blanket and pulled it over her shoulders. "Damn, it's cold in here. Nurse, can you please turn the air off?"

"I'm sorry, Denise. This hospital has central air. I'll bring you a few more blankets after I take your son for cleaning and blood work."

"Thank you."

"Not a problem, sweetheart."

"And thank you doctor for delivering my son," she added.

"I'm just doing my job, Mrs. Lambert. Now try to get some rest. You deserve it."

"So, Momma Di," Corey asked, "I was wondering... did Katrina hear such a wonderful prayer from you when she was born?"

"No, Corey, she didn't. But if I would have known she was going to become the little devil that she is, I would have given a full-blown sermon."

"I know that's right, Momma," Denise said. Her eyes

slowly closed and she began to fall asleep.

"Corey, did you and Denise decide on a name yet?"

"Yes, Momma Di. His name will be Malcolm, after the late Malcolm X Shabazz," Corey answered as he looked down at his son who was sleeping in a bassinet beside his wife. "I pray that someday you'll grow to be an even greater man than he was." Suddenly, his eyes filled with tears and they began streaming down his face. He lifted his son from the glass crib, pulled him to his face, and in a trembling voice whispered in his ear, "*Malcolm Curtis Lambert*, I love you."

"Okay, Mr. Lambert, it's time to take the little fellow away. He'll be back shortly for feeding time."

"It *is* pretty late. Corey, would you mind escorting an elderly woman to her vehicle?"

"Of course, Momma Di, but please give us a break with the 'elderly' act. You know you'd run circles around everyone in this room."

"You're right, child, just keeping you on your toes. Let's go, son. Denise, get some rest, honey," she said as she kissed her forehead, temporarily waking her. "You did an excellent job. I'll be back in the morning to check on you."

"You don't have to, Momma. Go home and rest. You *do* realize that you've been here during my entire eighteen-hour labor. If you're up to it, you can stop by tomorrow night. Trust me, Momma, we'll still be here. I don't think your grandson has any plans over the next few years."

"Alright, honey, try to get some rest and I'll call you tomorrow to see if you're in the mood for any visitors," she said as she left the delivery room.

"Yeah, try to get some rest, D. I need to hurry home to the kids. They probably have Brenda tied to a chair with wood burning underneath it by now. I'm just glad she's been

103

available to help out around the house. I'll see you tomorrow after work, okay?"

"Alright, honey. I love you."

"I love you, too, sweetheart. Goodnight."

"Goodnight, Corey."


"Brenda...Brenda, wake up."

"Oh...hey, Mr. Lambert. Darn, what time is it?"

"It's two a.m. How was everything?"

"Everything was fine until we decided to play Monopoly."

"Oh really, what happened?"

"Well, Kareem was winning, when Katrina got mad and beat him up. It didn't get too serious. I broke the fight up before it did. Kareem did get a scratch on his cheek, though. Katrina left after the fight and didn't return until midnight."

"What? Don't worry about it, Brenda. I'll take care of it in the morning. Were there any other problems?"

"No. Hey, how's Mrs. D?" Brenda asked as she sat up on the couch. "What did she have? What's the baby's name? How much did it weigh? How..."

"Whoa, slow down, Brenda. What the hell are you on? That's too much energy for someone to have at this time of the morning. First, she's fine and resting. Two, we had a boy. Three, his name is Malcolm. Four, he's eight pounds, two ounces. And five, I'm going to bed. Do you need a ride home or are you staying until morning?"

"My car's outside, but I'm too tired to drive, so I guess I'm staying, Mr. Lambert."

"Great. Well, you know the routine...make yourself at home," he said as he began to walk upstairs. "Damn that chick can talk," he mumbled to himself.

"Boy, that Mr. Lambert sure doesn't like to say much. Talk about Mr. Antisocial," she giggled as she tucked herself back onto the sofa. "And when are you guys gonna get a new couch? This one sucks!" she shouted. "You've had it for years!"

"There's always the front door!" he replied.

"Good morning, guys. Thanks for helping us to get ready, Brenda. I overslept just as I knew I would. Last night killed me. I feel as if I'd been partying all night. Wow, coffee! Guess you are good for something, huh, youngster?"

"That's very funny, Mr. Lambert," she said sarcastically. "I'm not a youngster anymore, did you forget? It's amazing how someone can fall asleep as a warehouse worker and wake up as a comedian. I don't think I know of anyone who can do that," she said as she put on her coat.

"Well, look at you. You've gone from nerd to Whoopee Goldberg overnight. I'm amazed myself. Congratulations," he said as he began to ruffle her hair.

"Touché, Mr. Lambert, touché. I've got to get going. I have a class at eight-thirty this morning."

"Have a good day at school, Brenda. Damn, how many more years do you have left? It seems like you've been in college for a decade."

"I graduate with a Masters this spring, thank God."

"Really? What's your major?"

"Psychology. I decided to stick with social sciences."

"Well I'm proud of you, Brenda. Take care of yourself, okay?"

"I'll try, Mr. Lambert. See you this afternoon."

"Alright, let's go, guys! We've got to get outta here!" he shouted from the front door as Katrina and Kareem ran down the stairs. "Oh yeah, Pumpkin, before I forget, I'm going to get straight to the point with this. Remember that little conversation that we had a couple of months ago about the whole 1-8-7 thing, dear?"

"Yes, Daddy."

"Good. Keep that in mind the next time you decide to put your hands on one of my children, okay?" he said as he kissed her on the cheek. "Now take your ass outside and get in the car before I decide to act out that little scenario to give you a better understanding."

"Yes, Daddy," she replied as she rapidly made her way down the front stairs.

"You, too, Mr. Innocent. Let's go."

"But, Daddy..."

"NOW!" he yelled.

Cory's relationship with Brenda was exactly what he always tried to build with Katrina. He would love to be able to joke with her as he did with Brenda. He knew he was the reason why Katrina behaved the way she did. He spoiled her for years, hoping that if he did, she would return her love to him by displaying excellent character. He often wondered where he went wrong. Corey left the streets alone many years ago, but the little he still had left in him, Katrina glorified. She noticed the respect he received whenever they went out and how even the toughest thugs showed him love. She felt his time in the streets must have been well spent to attain such an abundance of reverence, and therefore, she decided she wanted the same for herself. Little did she know, Curtis played a major part in her father's hierarchy.

His relationship with Kareem, on the other hand, was

the exact opposite. He didn't spoil him. In fact, he was hard on Kareem and didn't show him much attention at all. If not for Denise constantly mentioning it to him, he may have treated his son as if he were never alive. Although he tried to for many years, there was something that kept him extremely distant from his eldest son. He did want the best for him and loved him dearly, but didn't show it. You got it...no ball games or fishing for this little fellow, either. Just a 'good job' here and there, that was about it. Let's face it. He didn't know *how* to love a son. He was never shown how to. Or maybe it was something more serious than not knowing how to. Maybe it was something that festered deep inside and no matter how much he fought to ignore it, it always seemed to resurface whenever he dealt with his son. Only time would tell.

# CHAPTER
# 11

"Hi Den…" Corey said as he entered room 318. "Oh, I'm sorry. I'm looking for my wife, Denise."

"She's been moved to 304, down the hall," an orderly informed him as he removed a set of soiled sheets from the mattress Denise had slept on.

"Thank you," Corey replied as he left the room and proceeded down the hall.

"Hey Denise, is everything alright? Why were you moved?" he asked as he kissed her forehead.

"Everything's okay, honey. I was told that they needed the large room for a new patient, so they moved me into this smaller one. How are the children?"

"They're fine," he replied as he sat in a chair beside her. "Same shit, you know. Katrina beat on Kareem because he outdid her in a board game. I took care of it, though. How are you and Malcolm doing?"

"We're fine. They should be bringing him in to eat shortly. How was work today?"

"As usual, same shit different toilet." He paused for a moment. "Hey, do you remember Kimberly Watts?"

"Yeah, I remember her. Wasn't she called 'Ms. Easy' or something like that in high school? What about her?"

"She was hired as the new secretary at the warehouse

today. I just wanted to know if her name rang a bell."

"It did. Is there anything else that you think might *'ring a bell'* that you want to talk about?"

"No, I was just trying to strike up a conversation with you. Why are you getting so upset?"

"Corey, you know I never liked her. She was definitely the one person who would fuck your man in the blink of an eye. I don't understand why you would even bring her name up to me."

"Damn, Denise, my fault. That was so long ago I didn't remember. She's probably not even the same person she was in high school anyway. None of us are."

"Just drop it, Corey. Can you help me sit up, please? My back is killing me."

"Sure, no problem, baby," he said as he placed an extra pillow behind her neck. "Is that better?" he asked.

"Yes, thank you."

As Corey returned to his seat, a nurse entered the room pushing a plastic bassinet. "Good afternoon, Mr. and Mrs. Lambert. Here's your son."

"Oh my God, he's more handsome than I remember," Denise said as she reached out and took Malcolm into her arms. "Corey, pass me his blanket. I want to breastfeed him."

"That's one thing I've always admired about you, Denise. You've breastfed every one of your children. A lot of women don't practice that these days."

"When I was younger, my mother explained the importance of breastfeeding your children. It strengthens an infant's immune system better than formula does."

"Wow, my third child and I'm still learning something new about raising them each day."

"Hey, sis!"

"Tina...Jackie. What a surprise!" Denise said as she placed her hands in front of her mouth. Her overwhelmed reaction to their visit caused her eyes to fill with tears. "I didn't think I'd see you two until I got home."

"Aw, c'mon, girl. You know we wouldn't have missed this for the world. Is this the new addition to your family?" Tina asked.

"Yes, it is. His name is Malcolm."

"My God, he's adorable," Tina said as she reached out to gently caress his cheek. "He looks like your grandfather."

"I think I remember hearing my mother say that after I gave birth, but I'm not sure. I was kind of delirious at that point. Jackie, how are your children doing?"

"They're great, getting big, you know."

"Boy, do I. Pumpkin's big as a house and Kareem is catching up to her. How many do you have now? Ten, twelve?" Denise sarcastically asked with a smirk.

"Real funny, D. I have the same six that I've had for the last seven years. And, before you ask, Rodney and I are still together and doing wonderful."

"Who the hell is Rodney?" Tina inquired as if stunned that Jackie *ever* had a man.

"I told you guys about Rodney years ago. Remember?" Jackie softly replied, offended by Tina's question. "We were at the park after Curtis was murdered."

"I'm sorry, girl," Tina said as she put her arm around Jackie's shoulder. "I really can't recall a conversation concerning your relationships. I know we skimmed on the topic of how many children you had and all of their fathers, but that's about all I remember."

"Well, as I've said, my relationship with Rodney is

perfect and has been since we met."

"How *did* you meet? That is, if you don't mind me asking, Jackie," Denise asked as she wiped her milk from Malcolm's chin.

"No, I don't mind, Denise."

"Whoa, I'm gonna take this time to go and grab a soda or something while you three bump your gums," Corey said as he made his way toward the door. "I'll be back in a couple of minutes."

"I'm sorry, sweetheart. It's a girl thing, you know."

"Yeah, yeah, yeah."

"Anyway, Denise," Jackie continued after Corey left the room, "we met at the park. I'd taken the kids there one day after church to get some fresh air and there he was, sitting alone reading a book. I was surprised to see a young Black man reading by himself at a park, especially around here. I thought to myself, 'he's out of my league'. However, no sooner than the thought entered my mind, I saw him get up and begin to walk toward the bench that I sat on. He said he'd always admired a woman who spent quality time with their children and that what he'd seen reminded him of how his mother would take him and his siblings to the park after church when he was younger. Then, he politely asked if I was still with their father, or anyone else for that matter. I said no, he asked if he could sit with me, I said yes, and we've been together and in love ever since."

"Wait a minute," Tina said as she began laughing. "You mean to tell me that a young, and I'll assume handsome, brother walked up to you and your six children, said he admired what you were doing, and asked if he could sit and talk to you? Bullshit! You know damn well he wanted some pussy. He saw all of those children, noticed that none of them looked alike, and said, 'Fuck that, I'm next'."

"Tina, that wasn't nice," Denise snapped. "You get a kick out of hurting her feelings, don't you? Anyway, when was the last time you had some dick in your life?"

"That doesn't matter. I told you before, I don't need a man. A man can't do anything for me that I can't do for myself."

"Maybe that's 'cause won't no man put up with your conceited ass," Jackie said as she brushed past Tina and walked to Denise's bed. "Can I hold him, Denise?"

"Of course, Jackie. Have a seat."

"He is absolutely adorable. Too bad I won't be having anymore."

"Not that you need any," Denise said. "But why would you say that?"

"Rodney can't have any children, but always wanted them. I would have told you guys a second ago if Ms. *'Bourgeois'* wouldn't have interrupted me. *That* is why he was attracted to me, because I already had a family," Jackie said as she looked at Tina with a condescending expression. "And, by the way, we didn't have sex until six months after I met him."

"I'm sorry, Jackie. Maybe I did go overboard with what I said, but I love and care about you, and it aggravates me to see how you've destroyed your life by having all of these children at such a young age. I feel as though you had so much potential to be anything you wanted to be and you messed that up."

"But what you have to understand is that I didn't mess it up. When we were younger, you always said you wanted to be a big-time lawyer when you got older and you did, or at least you're on your way. If you think back to those days, you'll remember that all I ever spoke of was one day having a family with children to shower with love. Yes, I may not have done it the *'conventional'* way, but I did it and I'm very happy. Just as your job gives you a sense of being, so do my children. Now, God has blessed them with a loving father whose dreams are equivalent to mine where family is concerned. I no longer deal with their deadbeat dads nor do I want their support. Rodney makes more money than all of them put together anyway. He even asked me to marry him a week ago and I said yes. Meeting him is the reason why I've been practicing religion again so passionately. I've finally realized how much God loves me when he sent me his blessings in Rodney."

"Again, sis, I'm sorry and I'm very happy for you," Tina said as she walked to Jackie and embraced her. "Now, when were you gonna let us know?"

"I just did," she said with a smile as she handed Malcolm back to Denise.

"Boy, it seems like every time we're together, it gets serious. Speaking of we, has anyone seen Michelle?"

"I saw her about three weeks ago. She's not looking too well. I can't tell if it's the alcohol or what. She told me she lost her job and that she was staying with some nigga she's been seeing for a while. She appeared really depressed," Jackie voiced with concern.

"I haven't had time to cruise through the neighborhood lately," Tina interjected. "Work's been killing me."

"Well, when I'm feeling a little better, don't you guys think that maybe we should get together and become a little more involved in what she's dealing with? We are supposed to be best friends, aren't we?"

"She's right, Jackie. We're more like sisters, you

know."

"Yes, I know...sisters," she said as she grabbed their hands and began to smile.

"Are you girls still flappin' your yaps or is the coast clear?" Corey asked as he peeked into the room.

"Yes, Corey, we're done. Now come and hold your son while I go to the bathroom."

"No problem, honey. I know that you're not leaving me with the Witches of Eastwick, are you?"

"Oh, shut up, Corey," Tina said as she punched him on the shoulder.

"Hey! Watch my son and watch your hands. We're not children anymore, Tina. Shit, I'm a grown ass man now. I'll beat your athletic ass, girl," he jokingly stated as he took Malcolm from his wife. "Malcolm, make sure when you're older, you do a lot better than what you see in this room. But, if you're fortunate enough to find someone like your mother, I'll be very proud of you," he said as he stared into his son's eyes.

"Oh please, Corey, give it a rest. You *should* be hoping that he finds an educated Nubian queen such as me someday."

"You can't *spell* Nubian queen, Tina. Anyway, it seems to me that *no one* has been lucky enough to find you, from what I see."

"Whatever. Jackie, are you ready to leave? Suddenly this room has become a little overcrowded, don't you think?"

"You know, guys, no one can tell me that you two aren't brother and sister, or were in a past life. Yeah, I'm ready. Gotta hurry and get home to my family."

"Wow, I am so proud of you, girl," Tina commended

Jackie again. "You're really doing this family thing, aren't you? I know one thing, I better receive an invitation."

"Are you guys leaving already?" Denise asked as she came out of the bathroom. "You just got here."

"I know, Denise, but Jackie's gotta get home to her *fiancé.*"

"That's right, Tina," Denise replied. "We can't keep the lovebirds waiting now, can we? Congratulations, Jackie. You deserve it, girl." Denise slowly walked over to her longtime friend and embraced her. "Don't squeeze too tight, girl."

"Denise, here are a few things that Jackie and I picked up for our nephew. And, before you ask, the answer is yes. We are going to spoil him just like we spoil the other two, whether you like it or not," Tina said before kissing Denise on the cheek. "Love you, sis."

"You two are something else. Jackie, you really didn't have to. You should have spent your money on your children. I know it's gotta be difficult raising them."

"Not anymore. I already told you, *my Sweetie loves me.*"

"I think we get the picture, Jackie," Corey stated with a disgusted expression. "This has got to be the longest goodbye I've ever seen in my life. Jesus, leave already!"

"Oh, kill it, Corey. We're leaving. I'll call you tomorrow, sis. Take care of yourself, okay?" Tina said as she stuck her tongue at Corey and left the room.

"Betcha don't even know how to use it, lonely-ass!" he shouted as the door closed.

"See ya, Denise."

"Goodbye, Jackie. Kiss the kids for me."

"I sure will."

"Bye, Corey."

"Take care, Jackie."

"Corey, why do you give Tina such a hard time?" Denise asked as she returned to her bed.

"Because I love her, and that's how I show my love."

"As if I didn't already know. I do have to admit, though, I think the way you two interact is kind of cute. You don't have any siblings, and I guess if you did, you'd treat them the same way that you treat Tina."

"Yeah, maybe you're right. You know, growing up with you did have an impact on my relationship with Tina. You two lived together, and when you and I started dating, she looked at me as a brother. I guess she and I grew to love each other over the years just as you and I did."

"It sure looks that way."

"You know it's not right to have your mother waiting in a lobby while you and your little girlfriends sit around and cackle like a bunch of hens."

"Hi, Momma! We didn't know you were downstairs."

"Hi, Momma Di. Come have a seat. You look exhausted," Corey said before kissing her on the cheek and helping her sit down.

"You two know they have a 'three-person-to-a-room' policy around here. Show some consideration for the elderly. Is that my grandbaby? Bring him over here, child, so's I can see him."

"Here you go, Momma Di. Hey, look, he's finally opening his eyes again," Corey revealed with amazement.

"Aw, look at how he's staring at you, Momma. And he's smiling, too."

"Yes, he is. I think he's astounded by my beauty.

Never seen anything like it. Hey, little one. Oh, oh. What is that poking out on your face? Look at his lip. Oh no, he's frowning. I know he's not going to start cry…" Before Malcolm's grandmother could finish her sentence, he let out the most ear piercing sound she'd ever heard. "Alright, Denise, take him! You know your mother does not put up with crying babies. I thought I may have been able to get my hands on this one before you spoiled him, but I can see I didn't get here in time. Guess I'll have to try again with the next one."

"What next one, Momma? This is it!" Denise said as she lifted her son from her mother's arms. "You must be joking. I'm done. You hear me, DONE! When I leave this bed, Corey's lying on it to prepare for surgery," she said with a smile as she looked at her husband.

"What surgery? No one's going anywhere near these jewels, except for my wife. You best believe it."

"Well, if you *don't* wanna do anything, I guess sex in our home is about to become very scarce."

"Well, I guess it is then."

"You two mind having this conversation in the privacy of your own home?" Diana interrupted.

"I'm sorry, Momma. I just don't see me doing this ever again."

"Child, you've said that same sentence to me after every child you've borne. It's becoming a little redundant, don't you think, sweetie?" she said as she patted beads of sweat from her forehead with her handkerchief. "Why do you have the heat so high, Denise?"

"It's not me, Momma. It's this raggedy hospital. You freeze in the winter and cook in the summer. I mean, look at it. Same nasty aquamarine colored furniture that was here when I gave birth to Katrina thirteen years ago. The drapery hasn't changed much either if I recall properly. You know how they do in inner city hospitals. If I would have gone to the hospital in Eleven Oaks, I would have probably been able to request live entertainment in my room while I gave birth."

"I wasn't here when you gave birth to Katrina, but if I remember correctly, I'm willing to bet my next ten paychecks this is the same décor that was here when you had Kareem." Corey stood, walked over toward the window, and attempted to draw the drapes close. "Maybe if I block some of this sunlight, the room will cool off a little."

Are there more people and fewer hospitals in urban cities or less people and more hospitals in suburban America? Maybe more people become ill in urban cities and that explains why emergency rooms are always so overcrowded. Anyone who's ever been to one can attest to the 'take-a-number-and-wait' system that so many of these institutions utilize. It could be that there's less concern for the well being of those who may be less fortunate, and this accounts for the slow movement of the facility's personnel. Could be?

"It doesn't matter, Corey. I'll be out of here tomorrow morning. You just make sure everything is ready and packed so that we can leave here as quickly as possible."

"Hello, Denise. How are you feeling? My name is Dr. Tisdale. I just want to check your vitals and take some blood, okay? Is this your husband? If so, he's more than welcome to stay."

"Yes, it is, and this is my mother, Diana."

"Hello, Diana. What a beautiful name for such a beautiful lady."

"Hello, Doctor. May I inform you, charm will get you nowhere. Well, maybe a little," she said with a wink.

"Momma, stop it!"

"What, child? I'm old, not dead," she explained as she smiled at the doctor.

"Good afternoon, Mr. Lambert. Congratulations on your little one."

"Thanks, Doc. He's already turning out to be a bundle of joy," Corey said as he placed the sleeping infant back into his plastic bassinet.

"Well, let's have that arm, Mrs. Lambert. Just relax. This will only take a moment. Alright, now I need you to take a couple of deep breaths for me. Good. That does it, Mrs. Lambert. Now, if I'm not mistaken, you'll be leaving us tomorrow morning. Is this correct?"

"Yes, it is, Doctor."

"Great. The nurse will be here shortly to take your son back to the nursery. When she does, she'll have some literature for you to take home and a few papers for you to sign. The literature has some information that may benefit you."

"Okay, Doctor, have a good evening."

"I'll try. Hope to see you again, Mrs. Diana," he said as he looked past Denise to catch a glimpse of her mother.

"That all depends on what your work schedule entails, Doctor."

"MOMMA!!"

"You have a pleasant evening, Dr. Tisdale."

"You have a pleasant evening, also, Mrs. Diana," he said as he turned and exited the room.

"Momma, how could you?! Right in front of my face?! Daddy's body hasn't even fully decomposed yet and you're trying to date someone new."

"First of all, you lower your voice and show me

respect when you speak to me!"

"I'm sorry, Momma."

Corey's eyes nearly popped out of his head at the sight of how quickly his wife humbled herself. Although he remained quiet and dared not intervene, he devilishly thought to himself how he wished he had the same affect on her.

"Secondly, your father's been dead over twenty years now and I haven't looked at another man since his death. Believe me, child, he is about as decomposed as he's gonna get by now. I'm getting old and I'm lonely, Denise. Something you wouldn't understand because you've been too happy living your own life. Not that there's anything wrong with that, but you must understand, I need a life, too."

"Well, Momma, if you still cook the same way you always have, I'll leave my wife today and you'll never be lonely again. I promise," Corey interjected.

"Shut up, Corey. You're right, Momma. I was being selfish. Although it's been a long time since Daddy's death, I still find it difficult to imagine you with another man. I *was* 'Daddy's little girl', you know. Please forgive me for being disrespectful."

"I know, darling. You're forgiven. Corey, give me a hand, please. It's getting late and I want to get home and soak my greens for tomorrow. I'm making a welcome home dinner for the baby tomorrow, so make sure you invite all of your friends, alright?"

"All of them?"

"Yes, all of them."

"Thanks, Momma. I sure will."

"Yeah, thanks. That's really kind of you. C'mon, I'll walk you downstairs. That'll give us more time to discuss tomorrow evening's agenda, and the possibility of you and me hooking up someday," Corey said as he smiled and winked at his wife. "Goodnight, honey. I'll see you in the morning."

As Corey and his mother-in-law neared the elevator, Corey spotted Dr. Tisdale walking toward them.

"Good evening, Mr. Lambert, Mrs. Diana. I hoped I would see you again before you left, Mrs. Diana."

"Is that so, Dr. Tisdale?"

"Yes, I was wondering what *your* schedule *entailed* this weekend, if you don't mind me asking. That is, of course, if you are a single woman."

"Yes, Dr. Tisdale, I am a single woman, and I think my schedule is fairly vacant this weekend. Here's my number. Call me later tonight and maybe we can discuss this weekend in further detail."

"Sounds like a deal to me. Will eight o'clock be fine?"

"Yes, eight is perfect. I guess we'll speak then."

"I guess we will. Goodnight, Mrs. Diana, Mr. Lambert."

"Goodnight, Doctor," they said in unison.

As the elevator door opened, Corey whispered in his mother-in-law's ear, "Just don't let Denise find out, Momma Di. She'll kill both of us if she did."

"You're absolutely right, son. We'd better keep this one between us," she replied with a wink before kissing him on the cheek.

"MOMMY! I missed you. Is that my little brother? What's his name?" Kareem asked. His curiosity and excitement caused his eyes to illuminate the room.

"Hello, Kareem," she said as she kneeled down to kiss him. "I missed you, too. This is your brother, Malcolm."

"Hi, Malcolm. Wow, he's really wrinkled. What happened to his skin?"

"Nothing happened to his skin. Your skin looked similar to his when you were born. All babies do."

"Not *my* beautiful chocolate skin," he boasted.

"You've been listening to your mother too much, honey. Help your father bring the rest of the things in from the car for me. I need to sit down. I'm exhausted. Where is your sister?"

"She's upstairs talking to Brenda."

"Is she in trouble again?"

"No, not that I know of. Brenda just talks to her a lot about being a young lady and not a tomboy."

"Katrina! Mommy, Daddy, and Malcolm are home!" Kareem yelled before walking out of the front door.

"Hey, Ma, cute kid," Katrina said nonchalantly as she kissed her mother's cheek.

"Hi, Mrs. Denise," Brenda said. "Aw, he's gorgeous! He almost looks like a miniature Kareem."

"He does look a lot like his brother, doesn't he? The only difference is Malcolm has hazel eyes," Denise replied.

"Whoa, how did that happen?" Brenda asked.

"I've been asking myself the same thing," Corey said while trying to catch his breath. "Brenda, help me with these bags, please. After we finish with this, we're gonna take a walk and try to find that kid's father, Denise."

"Denying your child already, Corey? I thought you would have at least waited until he became a behavior problem."

"That was the old Corey. This Corey knows to get out as soon as possible, before it's too late," he joked as he placed her bags on the floor. "Now give me a kiss, baby."

"Don't 'give me a kiss baby' me, Corey. I'm keeping an eye on you."

"That's good. Then you won't miss me when I walk out of the front door and take that long stroll to get the kids some ice cream, now will you?" he said with a smile as he began walking upstairs.

"Don't play with me, Corey. If you try to leave us, I'll personally hunt you down, and I don't think you'll like what I'll do to you when I catch you."

Corey stopped halfway up the stairs and looked over the banister. "You must have forgotten who you're talking to. I know what you'll do to me, but what you don't understand is I might like it."

# CHAPTER
# 12

"Corey, can you get the ba..." Denise rolled over to nudge her husband, but realized he wasn't there. She peeked across the bed at the clock and noticed it was three-thirty in the morning. She forced herself to sit up and, with one eye open, scanned the bedroom attempting to locate him. She wasn't surprised to see him quietly sitting in a dark corner of the room with Malcolm lying on his shoulder. An empty feeding bottle rested between his legs as he tenderly tapped the infant on his back, hoping to burp him and put him back to sleep. The exhaustion in Corey's eyes was incredibly evident, but she refused to disrupt such a serene picture.

Malcolm was now four months old, and this morning was no different from the others. Corey faithfully jumped out of bed every morning since the birth of his son to change, feed, and put him back to sleep. Denise was amazed every time she witnessed it, as if it were the first time she'd seen it. Actually, it *was* the first time she'd seen it...with her children anyway. Corey never displayed such dedication with the first two children, which was exactly why he did it religiously with Malcolm. This would be the one who changed his life, and Corey chose to make sure he would be the best father he could be for him. It was his chance to start over. His bond with Katrina slowly diminished the older she became,

124

while his relationship with Kareem, or lack thereof, remained stagnant. This child would be different from the others, he promised.

Corey stood from the chair and gently placed his son back into the crib which sat beside them, before quietly tiptoeing back to bed.

"Are you all right, Corey?" Denise whispered as she snuggled beside him.

"Yeah. I'm sorry we woke you, D."

"Actually, you didn't. I lie here every night and watch as you perform your routine, and every night it amazes me. Why weren't you like this with the other children?"

"I don't know. All I know is that I want to do it with this one. Sometimes I feel like it's too late to repair what I have with the other two. With Malcolm, I feel like I've been given a fresh start to not make the same mistakes I've made with Katrina and Malcolm."

"Corey, as long as your children are alive, it's never too late. Every time you open your eyes in the morning, you've been blessed with the chance to make amends and better your life. You've always been an excellent father to these children. If you weren't, I wouldn't have continued having children with you. The older ones still need you. Katrina resented me at one time for showing Kareem more attention than I showed her. The reason I treated Kareem better was because I wanted to be a better mother and have a better relationship with him than I had with Katrina. Don't make the same mistake I made, Corey. Kareem already senses the distance in your relationship with him. Don't cause him to hate you and resent Malcolm by focusing all of your energy into Malcolm alone. I've been trying to rebuild my relationship with Katrina for years and it hurts like hell. Go to Kareem, Corey, and try to rebuild your relationship with him before it *is* too late."

Corey lay on his back, motionless, contemplating over Denise's words of wisdom. He slowly reached his hand across his stomach and searched for her hand. He found it and squeezed it tightly. "Thank you, D. I love you," he whispered.

"I love you too, Corey," she replied as she fell into a deep slumber.

# CHAPTER 13

## Corey:
## 5-24-96

"*D*enise, where's my other brown shoe?"

"Wherever you left it, Corey. I don't wear your shoes."

"Whatever, smart-ass," he mumbled as he lifted the sheets of the bed off of the floor to peek for the missing shoe. Just as Corey began to stand up, he felt a slight tug on one of his pants leg. "Denise, come and get Malcolm! I'm getting ready to leave and I don't have time to deal with him. Roman will be here in a minute. Where the hell is my goddamn shoe! Fuck it, I'll just wear the black ones. You can't find shit in this raggedy house anymore."

"Maybe if you helped a little more we could get some order around here," Denise snapped as she entered the bedroom and brushed past her husband to pick up Malcolm. "I don't know what's going on with you, Corey, but your attitude stinks! What is wrong with you?"

"Nothing, Denise. I just need to get out of this house," he said as he stuck his head out of their bedroom door. "Katrina, turn down that goddamn radio! See what I mean, Denise? It's total chaos around here. There're enough lights on in this house to brighten the whole damn neighborhood, and no one's occupying the rooms. Music blasting, babies crying, and where the hell is Kareem?"

"He's at the library," she replied.

"Oh yeah, he's at the library, as usual. Denise, it's almost eight-thirty in the evening. What the hell are we raising, a fucking rocket scientist?"

"You don't complain this much about Katrina, Corey, and she's *never* here. At least Kareem is doing something positive when he's not here and not hanging on some corner with a bunch of little gangsters."

"Yeah, and look at the little psycho chick now, Denise. She's in her room having her own personal party. Maybe she *doesn't* get out enough," Corey retorted as he opened his bedroom door. "Katrina, if I have to tell you to turn that music down one more time, I'm throwing you and your radio out of the window!"

"Corey, maybe you do need to leave. I didn't realize your home had become so miserable to you," she said as she sat on the bed with their son. "This drinking thing has totally changed you, Corey. Over the years, I've watched you fall deeper and deeper into the gutter right beside your foul mouth. I don't like it and I don't like that damn Roman, either. Don't get me wrong, Corey. I'm not blaming all of this on your friend. You're a grown man with a family, but lately, you've shown that a family is not what you want anymore. Go on and enjoy yourself, and take your time coming back. You won't be missed."

"Who said I was coming back?" Corey said as he grabbed his jacket, walked through their bedroom door, and headed downstairs.

As he reached the bottom landing, the front door opened. "Hey, Dad," Kareem nonchalantly greeted his father as he walked past him.

"Long time, no see, Einstein," Corey said as he left his home and slammed the door.

It had been over two years since the birth of Malcolm, and Corey's lack of self-worth began to take a toll on him. Corey was thirty-three now and he suddenly began to look at his life from a different perspective. Although he'd been working at the warehouse for almost a decade and became assistant supervisor during that time, he always reminded himself it wasn't his company and he could be laid-off or fired at anytime. He couldn't afford a new car and poor credit didn't make things any easier. The one he owned only had about five more miles left in it before its death. He'd just taken out a small loan on their home a few years ago in order to make repairs, and that did nothing but sink him into more debt. The anxiety had become insurmountable over the past couple of months and, during that time, he'd chosen the bottle as his savior. Many say that a Black man's midlife crisis usually begins in his early thirties.

"Hi, Ma. What's wrong with Dad now? Another tantrum or is he drunk again?" Kareem asked as he stood outside of his mother's bedroom.

"Watch your mouth, Kareem. You're being disrespectful. Your father is really stressed out. He won't talk to me, but he doesn't know how to solve his problems, either."

"I guess that makes it alright for him to treat us the

way that he does."

"I didn't say that. I'm trying to be understanding, but my patience is wearing thin. Why are you being so negative today?"

"I'm just tired of extending peace and getting none in return. We don't deserve this."

"You know, you're getting older, Kareem, and when this family experiences problems, I need you to be strong. I understand your frustration and I'm very proud of your schoolwork, but don't give up on your father so easily."

"I'll try, Ma. I'm going to lie down. I'm really beat and you know I have to be at the college tomorrow for that future entrepreneur seminar they're giving for the high school students," he said as he kissed his mother on the cheek. "I'll catch up with you tomorrow, too, lil' man." He smiled and lightly tapped his brother on the chin with his fist.

"I forgot about tomorrow, Kareem. You're not in high school yet. How did you get in?"

"My grades," he replied.

"Oh, excuse me, Mr. Smarty Pants. Goodnight, honey."

"Night, Ma. Night, Malcolm," he said as he left the bedroom.

"Corey!! The man's finally here. What's goin' on, bro? You're late."

"Hey, Rome. What's going on, fellas," Corey said as he exchanged handshakes and hugs. "I had trouble gettin' out tonight."

"Denise again?" Roman asked.

"Not really, I couldn't get my outfit together. What we drinkin'?"

"We're already on our third round, baby. This one's on you, Corey."

"No problem. Lord knows I need it. Hey, Chuck, a round of your finest cognac! Start a tab, alright?"

"You got it, Corey," the bartender replied.

Samuel's Pub, a.k.a. Sammy's, was known as the hot spot in the neighborhood. That is, of course, if you were considered a middle class resident. Middle class in urban areas means that you gross between thirty and forty thousand dollars a year. Every town has its sleazy go-go bars, desolate, smoke-filled watering holes, or virtually uninhabited hole in the wall saloons. But someone who hung out at a place like Sammy's wouldn't be caught dead in any of those places. Sammy's is for the working class only, and was well maintained to attract the type of crowd it did. Its atmosphere was very pleasant. Brawls, loud profanity, and lewd behavior were almost unheard of. The music was very tasteful, not deafening, and occasionally, local jazz bands would come to perform for a few hours in the evening. The façade, brick and highly polished oak, was detailed with brass trimmings, which made patrons feel as if they were among the elite of society. Wednesday nights were occupied by novice and veteran poets, which enticed neo-soul enthusiasts for miles.

Friday meant payday and payday meant 'drinks at Sammy's'. For Roman, it was routine, but for Corey, it would be the beginning of his downfall.

"Damn, you ain't bullshittin' tonight, are you?" Roman asked Corey, surprised his friend began ordering such strong drinks so early in the evening. "You alright?"

"I'm fine, and I'll be even better after about seven or so of these babies right here," Corey shouted as he raised his shot glass into the air. "Here's to gettin' fucked up beyond belief."

"Yeah, fucked up beyond relief," Roman hesitantly repeated.

Roman worked with Corey and became close friends with him over the years. Denise always felt he was a bad influence on her husband and blamed him for playing a major part in their marital difficulties. Actually, Roman's only problem was he didn't have a family of his own to take care of. His entire life was based on him. He moved there from California seven years ago and had no family, no wife, and no children. He worked, partied, never had a girlfriend long enough for anyone to have noticed, and basically took life one day at a time. Although this lifestyle made it difficult to relate to Corey's situation, he was beginning to notice a rapid decrease in Corey's attitude toward his family. When he and Corey first met, Denise and his children were all he talked about, but something more than a few drinks and a couple of nights of partying began to change that. For the first time, Roman actually found himself becoming concerned about someone other than himself.

"Alright Corey, let's not get too crazy too quick. The night's still young, bro," Roman stated, hoping it would slow Corey down.

"Naw, don't worry 'bout me, Rome. I've been looking forward to this night all week, and as excited as I am, I don't plan on prematurely shooting my load just yet," he said as he raised his shot glass to the bartender and gestured for a refill. "Three more of these and I'll slow down if that'll make you feel better, Dad."

"C'mon, Corey, it's not that serious, man. We're boys and I'm just watching your back, just as I know you watch mine, especially when we're out drinking."

"I feel you, Rome. I'm just a little stressed out and I need some R&R right now, not a lecture."

"Not a problem. Now how 'bout you buy me a beer?"

"Sure thing. Chuck, one on me for my man here," Corey shouted as he placed his arm around Roman's shoulder.

Suddenly, a soft and seductive whisper caressed Corey's ear. "I'll take an apple martini, thank you."

Corey immediately recognized the voice that almost caused him to forget who and where he was and instantly became infuriated.

"What the hell is she doing here?" Corey silently mumbled to Roman before turning his head to face the young lady who stood behind him. "Hey, Kimberly, what's up? What brings you here this evening?"

"I asked Roman if I could swing with you guys tonight, and he said it was cool. Do you have any protests?"

"No, not at all, Kim. Enjoy yourself. Rome, take a trip to the bathroom with me, alright?" Corey sternly requested.

"For what, man? You need me to make sure you don't pee on your nuts again?" Roman snickered as he high-fived his buddies.

"Stop fuckin' around and walk me to the bathroom, man."

"Alright, Corey, damn. What's the fuckin' rush? You need to slow down with your drinkin', man," Roman said as he swallowed the last of his beer. "You're really startin' to bug out."

"Drinking is not the problem right now, man. You are," Corey barked as he stood from his stool and left the bar.

As Roman began following Corey downstairs toward the restrooms, Corey suddenly stopped halfway down the second flight and turned to face him with a confounded expression on his face. "What the hell did you invite that bitch here for, man? All I need is for Denise to find out that she hung out with us at the bar tonight and I'll never hear the end of it. She already made a statement about her working at the same job as I do!"

"Whoa, slow down, Mr. Fuckin' Conceited. First of all, this isn't the first time that she's asked to come here, but it's the first time I said yes. Secondly, *I'm* trying to fuck her. That is, of course, if it's all right with you. Third, why in the hell do you even care who comes here anyway? I never knew you were so full of yourself, b."

"I'm sorry, man, my bad. It's just that my wife and I have known her for a while and she used to have a bad rep around the high school. A lot of folks used to say she'd sleep with a man even if they were taken. The fact that she was cool with his woman didn't matter at all. I also heard she was easy prey. Not that it means she still is."

"Well, let's just hope for my sake that she *still is*. You know what I'm sayin', bro?" Roman began laughing and lightly punched Corey on the shoulder.

"Yeah, yeah, yeah. I hope you don't think you're going to retain her attention with that clown suit you're wearing."

"What's wrong with my suit? This is what's happening."

"No, that's what was happening to pimps over ten years ago. C'mon, man, SHARKSKIN!" Corey exploded with laughter as he began to rub the sleeve of his comrade's jacket. "Gators, yes. Sharkskin? Absolutely not! This is almost the new millennium, b. Catch up."

"I'm not hearing you right now, Corey. Look at you, you have *no* sense of fashion whatsoever. Your get-up has been the same since the day I met you. T-shirt and jeans, t-shirt and jeans. Shit ain't changed in five years and you have the audacity to comment on *my* attire? I'm surprised you're even wearing slacks tonight. Nigga, you don't know shit. These hoes love the way I get down. What the fuck does your old monogamous ass know about these bitches anyway? If it wasn't for me hangin' out with your lonely ass, you'd think all women looked like Denise."

Although Roman was only teasing Corey, the comment about him being lonely and only knowing of Denise when it came to women did strike a nerve. No man wants to have the title of being *"pussy whipped"* hanging over his head. The next thing Corey had to do was figure out a way to defend himself without disrespecting his wife and without hitting Roman below the belt.

"Dig, man. We're in our thirties now, you know what I'm sayin'? I don't think there was anything wrong with me settling down and doing the right thing years ago, you feel me?"

"Naw, not really, bro. These chicks call themselves hoes and bitches all the time, and we're supposed to respect them? I don't think so. That's why I ain't settled down with one of 'em yet, because every one I've ever met had low self-esteem 'bout themselves. Why should I respect that? Now *that* little honey who came here tonight, she's gettin' it next. I hear she likes to fuck, and so do I. So, if you're done bullshitting with me, I would like to get back upstairs and finish filling Kim with liquor so that I may possibly fulfill my aspirations of waking up next to her with a crusty penis in the morning. Now, are you feeling *me*?" he arrogantly boasted with a grin.

"Well, don't let me stop you, bro. You know, between me and you, I kinda envy you. I can't even remember what it feels like to be with another woman. I've been faithful to my wife for over a decade now, and although I've had the opportunity to stray, I never have and I doubt I ever will. I love my wife, even though I feel like choking her ass at times. That probably goes both ways though, huh? Keep what I said on the low, alright? I don't want these niggas in my business. You know they can go overboard at times."

"No problem, man. C'mon, let's head upstairs. The next round's on me," Roman said as he placed his arm around Corey's shoulder and attempted to put him in a headlock.

"Whoa, slow down there, big man. Don't make me bust yo' ass in here," Corey stated as he pulled himself from Roman's clutch. "I ain't that drunk."

"What the hell took you two so long?" Kimberly inquired. "What were you doing, jerkin' each other off?"

"Naw, I'm saving that job for you, babe," Roman said as he kissed Kimberly on the top of her head. "Chuck, one for me and my man, okay?"

"No problem, Rome," the bartender replied. "You know, that little lady of yours sure can put 'em down. She's had three martinis between the time you guys left and now," Chuck said as he placed their drinks in front of them.

"Oh, is that so? And at whose expense?" Roman asked as he looked at Kimberly.

"At your expense, Rome. Is there a problem? You *did* invite me here tonight. The least you can do is hook me up with a couple of drinks."

"And what's in it for me, if you don't mind me

asking?"

Kimberly stood from her stool, seductively positioned herself behind Roman's seat, and softly whispered, "Only time, and a few martinis, will tell."

One thing was true. Kimberly Watts had been very promiscuous in the past, and yes, she still was. Roman would be another notch under her belt, and if *he* wasn't, it would have been anyone who delighted her eyes that evening.

Kimberly was very attractive. She was what African-American males referred to as a redbone. The problem with Kimberly wasn't that she was a slut, but the fact that her motto was "do as men do". Everyone knows that society makes it acceptable for a man to sleep with as many women as he wants to and he's still considered a man. However, if a woman does the same, then she's labeled as a slut. Kimberly didn't care what people thought of her, though. What was good for the goose was good for the gander. Many men attempted to get her into bed and, after achieving their goal, were left alone and distraught wondering what they'd done to lose her. It's not a good feeling to have sex with someone and, after one glorious night of passion, your phone calls are not returned. It doesn't matter if you're male or female, the feeling is mutual.

"I don't feel too well, bro. I think I might have overdone it," Roman said before holding a napkin to his mouth. "I should have eaten first."

"Damn, Roman, it's only ten o'clock! You talk all that shit 'bout being *'the man'* and you can't even hang. I thought I was the one who was new to this," Corey replied.

"Naw, it ain't that. I'm tellin' you, I didn't eat before I left the house and now the liquor ain't sittin' right. I need to get outta here and get some air."

As Roman continued making excuses for his drunken state, Kimberly's facial expressions began to show signs of disenchantment. "Are you trying to tell me that you invited me out for drinks and now you're leaving? Whatever happened to our night out?"

"It's not like that, Kim. I, uh...uh...Oh shit!" Before Roman could finish his sentence, he found himself spreading his legs, placing his head between them, and liberating half of what he'd recently devoured at the bar.

As Roman spewed what was irritating his stomach, three of his cronies simultaneously released beer and chuckles from their mouths.

"Yeah, homie, who's the bitch now?" Corey blurted with tears in his eyes. "And you had the audacity to tell *me* to take it easy."

"Rome!" Kimberly yelled. "You almost got it on me! I don't believe you did this!"

"I'm sorry, Kim," Roman slurred. "Hey, can one of you guys drive me home? My head's really spinnin'."

"Yo, I'll run you home, but I have to drive your car," Simon volunteered. "You live right around the corner from my girlfriend's house. I'll walk there from your crib after I drop you off. I told her I'd be there early tonight after I stopped for a few drinks, so I know she's probably waiting up for me."

"I really appreciate it, man. Kim, are you coming?"

"I don't think so. For what? A drunk fuck?"

"Actually, that's *exactly* what I was thinking," he said as he leaned on her.

"You know, Rome, you're nothing that I expected you to be." She brushed him from her shoulders.

"Well, will you at least walk me to my car?"

"Walk you? How 'bout you walk your damn self. I can't believe you, Rome. You put on this show like you're some kind of player when, in fact, you're a big ass joke."

"Wow, I guess I deserved that," he slurred. "I can see that you're a little upset with me right now, so I guess this means I have to wait until tomorrow to sleep with you, huh?" he said as he put on his jacket. "Whatever. Hasta mañana, people."

"Yeah, try to get some rest, bro. I'll give you a ring tomorrow morning to check on your hangover," Corey said as he stood to embrace Roman.

"A couple of aspirin and a cold beer when I wake up will take care of that. I'll see you guys later. Goodnight, Ms. Watts," Roman said with an arrogant smirk.

"Goodnight, Mr. Disappointment," Kimberly replied.

The evening ensued. There was a lovely cocktail of ambiance, good drinks, and good people, and for a moment, it seemed as if the world stopped. Sammy's was packed with the afterwork mob meeting for a little down time before heading home. Before long, it shifted to the late crowd dressed to impress and hoping to meet someone for life at best, or just for the night at worst. They laughed and drowned their sorrows, frustrations, and issues in good company and drinks and food in a place comfortable enough to relax and unwind without worrying about first impressions and façades. The next thing they knew, the crowd at the bar thinned to those last few who couldn't get lucky even if their life depended on it, shared by those who needed the drink for survival. Finally, Corey and his cronies were met with an ill-timed last call for alcohol which left them with overwhelming bar bills, fatigue, and blood alcohol contents of 3.0 and higher.

"Corey, I think it's about time for you to get out of here," Chuck stated as he wiped a wet cloth across the bar. "Looks like you're done for, buddy."

"Yeah, I'm pretty fucked up, man. I can't even keep my eyes open. It's cool, though. I live just a few blocks from here. What do I owe you, Chuck?" Corey mumbled as he reached for his wallet.

The bartender casually slid a receipt under Corey's coaster.

"Here you go, Chuck. Keep the change, alright?"

"Thanks, Corey. Try to get home safe."

"Are you sure you'll be okay?" Kimberly asked. "Where's your car?"

"It's outside. I'll pick it up in the morning or send Denise to get it," Corey answered as he stood from his stool.

"I can run you home if you like," she offered.

The suggestion caused Corey to momentarily become sober. "Are you out of your fuckin' mind? Denise would have a fit if I pulled up to our house with you in the car."

"Why?"

Suddenly, Corey began to feel as if he'd just opened a can of worms. "Uh, I don't know. You know how jealous wives can be."

"Well, from what I see, she has many reasons to feel that way," she softly said as her eyes began to wander over his body. "C'mon, I'll drop you off around the corner from your house, if that'll make you feel better."

"I don't know, Kim."

"Let's go, wimp. Don't worry, I promise not to bite."

"You're right," Corey said as he stumbled back onto his seat. "I can barely walk anyway. I don't know who I thought I was fooling."

"That's more like it," Kimberly said as she grabbed Corey's arm and lifted him from his seat. "Damn, I see someone definitely works out. I never knew your arms were so huge," she whispered. "Goodnight, everyone. It was nice hanging out with you guys. I hope we can do this again one day. C'mon, Corey, help me out a little. You have to at least take steps on your own and I'll support you."

"What you say? I'm cool. I got it. Alright, fellas, I'll catch up with y'all later," he stammered.

# CHAPTER
# 14

"*D*amn, Denise, that feels so good. You didn't even wait for me to wake up and take my clothes off," Corey silently slurred. "Whoa, slow down some. I'm still a little fucked up. Where's Malcolm?"

"Who's Malcolm, Corey?"

Corey slowly opened his eyes, praying to God he didn't hear correctly the question that had just been asked. "WHAT THE FUCK ARE YOU DOIN'?!!"

"What's wrong, baby? Did I bite? I know I promised not to," Kimberly answered as she lifted her head from between his legs and slowly wiped her bottom lip with the back of her hand. "I thought you wanted me to slow down."

"Aw, hell no, Kim! This is fucked up and you know it!" Corey said as he fumbled for the handle to the car's door. "Why are you doing this?"

"You were asleep and I couldn't resist," she jokingly replied.

"Where are we? Shit, I don't believe this. I've gotta get the fuck outta here."

"Okay, wait, Corey. I was kidding. I…"

"About what Kim, sucking my dick?! Why, Kim?"

"Alright, let me just say something to you and then you can go. Please, just give me a couple of minutes, okay?"

142

"You've got two, so use 'em wisely, Kim."

"Corey, I've wanted you since high school. And I don't just mean sexually, either. I really wanted you like a wife wants her husband, but you never paid any attention to me. All you ever wanted was Denise, and what did she give you in return? A child that's not even yours, that's what. For years I sat and watched you put all of your energy into her and her daughter. I would have *never* done that to you. I've always felt you deserved better than that."

"Oh, I get it. So you wait for over a decade to show me how much you care by giving me head, right? Get a grip, Kim."

"No, Corey, that was a mistake. Just listen to me for a moment, please. I've always loved you. I know that I've been very promiscuous for many years, and I realize it's because I've been trying to fill a void I know belongs to you. I wanted my first child to be *our* first child. Denise didn't even love you enough to take that thought into consideration."

Kimberly's words began to slowly release a demon that Corey had been keeping suppressed for many years. The same demon that almost caused him to chip a tooth one hot summer day upon returning from an interview some time ago. The same demon that resurfaced periodically to manipulate him into unintentionally starting arguments with his wife. The same demon that walked him to Sammy's every week and shared drinks with him. And, obviously, the same one that just left him passed out in the passenger seat of Kimberly's car. What a setup.

As Corey sat and stared through the windshield at a flickering streetlight, Kimberly noticed his hand slowly fall from the door's handle and back onto his lap. It became difficult for her to decipher if the expression on his face was one of rage or sorrow.

"Are you alright, Corey?" she asked as she grabbed his hand.

"All these years I've tried to endure the trials and tribulations of keeping what I've felt like I'd always wanted, a family with Denise," he responded without taking his eyes away from the pulsating, faded yellow streetlight. "And all these years what you just said has always haunted me. Deep down inside I've always felt it, the hatred toward Denise for having Katrina by a man other than myself. I love that woman more than anything, and I love our daughter. But my blood doesn't run through her veins. Some people say that it doesn't matter, but they're not in the same situation to understand. Maybe it's Satan that makes me feel this way. Whatever it is, it drives me crazy sometimes. You're right, though, Kim. I did want my first child with Denise to be *our* first child, and she's not."

"Then give me that, Corey. Give me my first child and let it be *ours*," she coaxed as she lifted her leg over his lap and began to straddle him. "That's what I've always wanted from you. Please, give me your child."

Corey's heart told him to push her back into her seat and run like hell, but his head, the little one, didn't allow that to happen. He knew the last thing he ever wanted to be labeled as was a "baby's daddy", and if he went through with this sin he was minutes from committing, he would take care of his responsibility not only financially, but physically as well. That wasn't the question at this point. The problem was alcohol! You know, the thing that makes you oblivious to the question of whether or not someone has AIDS before you have unprotected sex with them. It has also been known to provoke men into thinking with the wrong head at times and even cause people to appear to be a lot more attractive than they actually are. Top this off with a beautiful, golden cleavage dancing in front of your face along with a gyrating pelvis on you lap, and the "Just Say No" slogan will quickly begin to fritter away.

More importantly, if he was sober, he would have seen how this was the root of his dilemma. At some point, Katrina's biological father had become a "baby's daddy", and he knew after he did this, there was the possibility he'd also be one. There was no way he'd leave his family for this woman, no matter how alluring she was.

"Corey, forget about what she's done to you," she whispered between gentle, seductive kisses on his earlobe. "Forget the pain of not being the father of her oldest child, and be the father of mine. Right here, baby, just like this."

For a moment, Corey sat motionless, perplexed and inebriated. The longer he mulled over the statements Kimberly deceitfully used to entice him, the more she seemed to make sense. And the more sense she made, the more infuriated he became with that which had been long forgotten. Suddenly, everything became clear. She was right! He *didn't* deserve what had happened to him. He *should* father a child with a woman who had no previous children from another man. Shit, this woman *did* express true love and loyalty for him from the very beginning. Hell, she *is* better than what he had at home.

Or maybe it's just Mr. Demon again, with an ice cold brewsky for his pal.

"Alright, that's what you want, Kim," he growled in a sinister tone. "You want it right here...like this?" He placed his right hand on her throat and pushed the back of her head against the dashboard, causing her back to arch and become trapped between the realms of pain and pleasure, while simultaneously unzipping his pants to reveal a forced eruption of desires. As he fervently thrust himself inside of her and tore open her blouse, he tightly clenched his teeth and grunted, "Is this what you want, Kim? You want me to cum inside of you…"

# CHAPTER
# 15

"*C*orey, wake up, honey. I made breakfast for you. You look terrible." Denise sat on the bed against Corey and held a plate of pancakes, eggs, and bacon in front of his face. "I poured some orange juice for you and brought you some aspirin. You look as if you might have a hangover."

Although Corey heard what was being offered to him, he remained motionless, slightly confused as to whether last night really existed or if it had been just another intoxicated wet dream. He didn't open his eyes nor did he say anything, terrified that if he responded, it may not have been his wife who answered him *again.*

He decided to play it safe. "What did you say? My head is pounding."

"I can tell. That's why I made something for you. I've never seen you this hung over before. I'll just put it on the nightstand until you're ready for it, okay? I have to go and feed the children."

Alright, the coast was clear. Kimberly didn't have any children to feed, so he must have been home. Corey slowly opened his eyes just in time to catch a blurred image of Denise exiting the bedroom. It was hard for him to differentiate what was more painful: the hammering sensation inside of his head, the rays of the sun which peeked through the Venetian blinds and charred his retina, or the guilt of what he did the night before.

He sat up, positioned his back against the headboard, and placed the palms of his hands over his forehead. "Corey, what the fuck have you done?" he asked himself.

As the bedroom began to spin, the antipathy he felt for his sins not only began to ruin his appetite, but caused what was left of his previous meal to resurface...all over his breakfast.

"Goddamn it! What the fuck! D! D, can you come upstairs!" he shouted.

"What's wrong, Corey?" Denise asked as she burst into their bedroom. "Why are you shouting? What hap...? Corey, what the hell is wrong with you?! Was last night so intense that you had to wake up and vomit all over the place?"

"Intense? What are you talkin' about, Denise? Was what intense?" he quickly babbled, wondering if she was hiding something she knew from him.

"Nothing. It just seems as if you may have had *too* much fun last night. Why? What did you think I meant?"

Corey decided to think this time before responding, realizing he'd almost spilled the beans on himself. "I just thought you were trying to be funny, that's all. You know you can be facetious at times," he responded, the guilt eating at his soul like acid. "I'll be okay, though. Maybe I just need a cold shower or something."

"Maybe," she said as she turned to walk away. "I'll be back, baby. I'm going to get a rag and some water to clean this up."

"Denise, wait."

"What's wrong?"

"Nothing. I just wanted to tell you that I'm sorry for last night. Lately, I've been acting like an ass and I've been fucking up a lot. I can't live like this anymore. I don't want to continue to have a relationship with you like we've been having. I want the old us back. I've been stressed out and acting erratically lately. One thing I've realized is that I have to start praying again and asking for guidance or else we're not going to make it."

Denise stood stationary and listened to her husband's confessions.

"And yes, before you ask, I'm still a little fucked up. But I don't want you to think that has anything to do with this revelation I'm having right now," he said.

Actually, he wasn't lying. What he did with Kimberly was literally tearing him apart. The more he reminisced about his previous evening, the more he hated himself. Where were all of those thoughts stemming from and how was he so easily manipulated? Corey always knew the grass was never greener on the other side, but for some reason, he took a chance on his family anyway. One thing was certain...he would never drink again if he got through this in one piece.

"Denise, I need a few more hours of sleep before I get up."

"Corey, I've never cared about what time you get up on the weekend, so why do you suddenly feel as if you need to tell me what time you're getting up?" she replied as she left their bedroom

"Well, if you'd let me finish, I was going to ask you if you had any plans tonight."

"Why?" she called out from the hallway.

"I thought maybe we could catch a movie or dinner or something. We haven't been out in while. I thought maybe we could use it."

"Well, why can't we do both?" she asked as she peeked her head back inside the doorway of the bedroom. "Are you alright, Corey? You're acting a little strange."

"Yeah, I'm fine. I just miss the old days, that's all," he said as he began to climb out of bed. "Don't worry about this mess, D. I'll clean it up."

"Are you sure, Corey? You know, you're not looking too well."

"I'm fine. Just got a few things on my mind, that's all."

"Wanna talk about it?"

"Not really. I just need some time to pull myself together."

If there was one thing certain about Denise, it was the fact she was far from being stupid. Although she only patronized Corey by entertaining him with the conversation she just had with him, she didn't forget about the argument which took place the night before. She also had a gut feeling that something happened while he was away from home. She just prayed it had nothing to do with promiscuity.

# CHAPTER
# 16

"*Y*ou guys come downstairs and eat!" Denise shouted. "And make sure you wash your faces and brush your teeth before you do."

"Good morning, Denise," Corey said as he entered the kitchen and attempted to adjust his tie. "I don't have time to eat anything. I have a meeting this morning. I'll just grab a coffee on my break later on." He leaned forward and kissed her forehead. "You guys have a good day at school. By the way, Denise, this has been one of the best weekends I've spent with you in a long time," he whispered in her ear. "Oh, and, Kareem…"

"Yes, Dad?" he dispassionately replied.

"Will you be home early tonight?"

"Probably. James is sick, so I don't have anyone to study with. Why?"

"Thought maybe you might like to go a few rounds on the basketball court tonight."

"I guess so. That would be cool," he responded, astonished his father remembered how to speak to him in such a peaceful tone.

"Alright, see you then. Take care everybody."

"See ya, Dad," Katrina said, thrilled to see the old

Corey back.

"Bye, Da Da," Malcolm blabbered.

"Oh my God! Corey, did you hear that?!"

"I heard it, Denise, I heard it," he said with a smile as he rushed across the kitchen, picked his son up, and cuddled him. *"I can't believe I almost destroyed this,"* he thought to himself.

"...and if we follow these few simple steps, we should be able to increase production by a minimum of ten percent. Thank you for your time. Now let's get back to work," Corey said while turning off an overhead projection. "Can someone turn on the lights on their way out, please? Thanks." As Corey gathered the rest of his paperwork, he noticed Roman approaching him from the other end of the conference room.

"Corey, you got a minute?"

"Yeah, Rome, what's up, man?"

"Did you hear about Kim?"

The sound of her name caused the butterflies in Corey's stomach to swell and almost erupt. "No, what happened?"

"She called the manager in human resources and told her that she wouldn't be returning to work. She said she was offered a new job and that she'd be catching a flight this afternoon to finalize her contract."

"Contract? I thought she was just a damn secretary. What type of company is she going to work for where you need a contract?"

"I don't know, but from what I heard, this place was just a stepping stone for her. Word is she had a pretty serious portfolio. I don't know why she ever took this job in the first place."

Roman may not have known why, but Corey had a

pretty good idea. "I didn't hear anything yet, man, but if I do, I'll let you know."

"Really? That's funny because she called me on Saturday and told me she gave you some before you got home that morning," Roman said with a bewildered expression.

"What!" Corey whispered, "She told you?"

"Look, it's nothin', man. It ain't like I'm some kind of bitch or anything. All's fair in war and pussy, right?" Roman stated with a smile.

"I guess so."

"Well, let me get back to work, Mr. Boss Man," Roman said as he began to leave the conference room.

"Whoa, where is this 'boss man' shit comin' from, Rome?"

"Nowhere. I'm just acknowledging that you're the man, that's all," he replied without turning to look at Corey.

Corey remained motionless and speechless as Roman left the room. For the first time, he questioned the sincerity of their friendship. Roman *was* a "player'", so to speak, but even a player, no matter how well they performed the charade, has feelings. The attitude Roman just displayed was enough to confirm that.

# CHAPTER 17

# Denise:
# 12-6-97

"*D*enise, I've gotta get out of here, baby. I'm late as hell. I'll call you at your office, okay?" Corey said as he grabbed his briefcase and headed for the front door.

"Wait, Corey, don't tell me you forgot already," she said as she seized him by the forearm.

"Forgot what?" He paused for a second before dropping his briefcase. "Aw shit, Katrina's meeting is this morning, isn't it? No problem, let me try to contact Frank and inform him that I'll be late. Where is she anyway?"

"She walked to school with her buddies, as usual. I swear I am so sick of dealing with her."

"You and me both," he replied as he reached for his belt and unhooked his cell phone. "The sad thing is she doesn't realize that her friends don't respect her, but fear her. If she hadn't become the notorious demon-seed that she is, those

154

same kids who claim they'd go through the fire for her would be chasing her home or kicking her little punk ass everyday," he said before grabbing her hand and escorting her toward the front door.

"I know that's right," she said before joining his laughter.

"Good morning, Mr. and Mrs. Lambert. Won't you have a seat, please?"

"Thank you," they replied in unison. Corey pulled out a seat for his wife before sitting down.

"Hello, my name is Mrs. Prescott, and I am the vice-principal," she said as she reached over her desk to shake Denise's hand. "Let me first start by apologizing for the inconvenience. I know both of you have jobs you must attend to, but I didn't think there was any other way of resolving the problems that have been occurring lately here at the high school."

"Believe me, Mrs. Prescott, we understand," Denise interjected before cutting an eye to Katrina, who sat in a corner of the office. The blasé attitude Katrina displayed did not assist in deescalating the boiling point her mother was only seconds from reaching.

"First, I would like to address our most vital issue… Katrina's gang affiliation."

"What!" Denise shrieked as she looked at Katrina. "What gang affiliation is she talking about, girl?! Answer me before I choke the…" Denise stood from her seat and began walking toward her daughter.

"Calm down, Denise," Corey interrupted as he grabbed her wrist and pulled her back into her seat. "Let Mrs. Prescott finish, honey," he said before glancing over his shoulder and giving Katrina a sinister grin. Although he pretended to be calm, his first reaction was to do a favor for the janitor of the school by mopping the vice principal's floor with Katrina's back.

"Thank you. Alright, where was I? Yes, Katrina's gang activities have become a major issue. Now, the reason you've been asked to appear for this meeting is because we've recently been informed that your daughter is not just affiliated with the infamous female gang 'K.O.Q.', also known as the 'Knock Out Queens', but she's also the leader. As you may already know, K.O.Q. is the number one female gang in the state."

"Excuse me?!" Denise said as she attempted to wiggle her hand from Corey's grasp. "And when did this happen, if you don't mind me asking?"

"Well, that's just it, Mrs. Lambert. She's the leader because she's the founder."

"Oh, this just keeps getting better and better, huh?" By now, she'd found a way to free her hand and fully turned herself around to face her daughter. "Well, what do you have to say for yourself, Mrs. Corleone?" she asked. Now, what Katrina didn't realize at this point was this is where a parent's deceit begins to take place.

For some strange reason, children have been duped into believing once their parents reach the age of thirty, they become part of that well-known group of people known as *"over the hill"*. You see, Denise's plan at the time was for Katrina to *think* her mother was going to behave in a disciplined manner. You know, show some panache, so to speak. Suddenly, out of nowhere, that little fellow known as Mr. Ego caused a *"what are you gonna do about it"* expression to appear on Katrina's face. Poor girl never even saw what was coming.

"Are you going to answer me or..." Before Denise could finish her sentence, tunnel vision unexpectedly set in. The only thing her eyes were able to focus on was the tough-girl appearance which seemed to be glued to Katrina's face. Denise felt one of her eyebrows slowly rise and her head began to slowly tilt to one side. She began to experience a warm sensation developing behind her ears, followed by slight twitches in her right eyelid. Suddenly, without warning and without senses, Denise sprung from her seat, hurdled two chairs, and leaped ten feet across the room and onto her daughter's throat. If her actions would have been scored on performance and agility, she would have received a perfect ten.

"Oh my God!" Mrs. Prescott yelled.

"D, don't!" Corey shouted, jumping from his seat. As he made his way to his daughter's rescue, he began wondering to himself, *"How in the hell did she get over there that fast?"*

"I'll kill you! I swear to God I'll kill you, girl!"

Katrina screamed with veins protruding from her forehead.

"I am so tired of you!" Tears began to flow from Denise's eyes.

Corey wrapped his arms around Denise's waist and pulled her off of Katrina. "That's enough, Denise. That's enough," he whispered in her ear before escorting his kicking wife back to her seat.

Katrina lay motionless in a fetal position trembling and whimpering, "I'm sorry, Momma. I'm sorry."

As Corey guided his enraged, sobbing wife back to her seat, he looked over to Katrina, who was still curled in a ball gasping for air, and shook his head.

"My apologies, Mrs. Prescott, I don't know what came over me," Denise explained as she fixed her hair and wiped tears from her face. "Please continue."

"Well, Mrs. Lambert, I don't think there's much left to say," she replied with a smirk. "Looks like you've said it all. I *do* think it would be better if Katrina left with you for the day, though. Maybe you three can take some time to sort this out."

"I think that's an excellent idea," Corey stated as he stood to put on his coat. "Thank you for your patience, Mrs. Prescott."

Normally, Corey would have been the one who reacted irately, but he decided to sit this one out for a few reasons. One, it was too early in the morning for any drama. Two, Katrina had this coming for some time, and three, why should he get his hands dirty when Denise was doing such a terrific job of handling this herself.

"Yes, thank you," Denise said as she extended her hand towards the vice-principal. "And again, please excuse my behavior."

"Don't worry about it, Mrs. Lambert. Trust me, I understand. Not only do I have two teenagers of my own, but I've also been working with teens and gang related issues for many years. I couldn't begin to imagine receiving news that one of my children was involved in gang activities."

"We thank you for being understanding," Corey stated. "We'll see what we can accomplish from our end, but we'd appreciate it if you would incorporate some type of intervention within your educational program that would assist us in dealing with Katrina and her disciples."

"It's funny you requested that, Mr. Lambert. It just

so happens my staff and I just recently sat with the chief of police to discuss different methods of not only dealing with gangs, but also putting an end to the outbreak of gang activities within our neighborhood."

"That's very comforting," Denise added. "If you have any more problems or questions, please feel free to contact me or my husband at home or at work."

"Absolutely, Mrs. Lambert, and again, thank you for your time," she said as she stood from her desk.

"You're welcome, Mr. Prescott," Denise said. "Have a wonderful day."

"Yes, have a wonderful day," Corey added.

# CHAPTER
# 18

*A*s Denise and Corey left the building, they both wondered what the conversation on their way home would consist of.

"Mommy…"

"Don't say a word, Katrina. I am so disappointed in you right now. How could you? How could you take everything that your father and I taught you and just throw it in the garbage? For years, I slaved to get an education and worked my ass off to give you and your brothers a better life. I've set example after example for you, and this is how you repay me? You just remember that what you do today will come back on you tomorrow. We call that karma, Katrina." Karma or not, Katrina couldn't have cared less. The only regret she had at that moment was getting caught.

The K.O.Q. were very well known and feared even more than their popularity suggested. Corey and Denise heard of the gang on more than one occasion but were oblivious to their activities. You see, when parents reach a certain age and level of professionalism, they tend to separate themselves from the ongoing realities their children face on a daily basis. The problem is not that they don't want to be familiar with where they came from. They just believe what their generation experienced in the streets was the truth, and anything that came after them was nothing more than a defective carbon copy. The truth of the matter is the streets are still the streets. Over decades, thugs have graduated from using rusty knives to rusty razor blades and now, rusty guns. The stage *never* changes, just the actors. Weapons are still weapons and killers are still killers, regardless of what "year" it is.

"Corey, would you mind making sure she gets home? I have a doctor's appointment early this afternoon."

"No problem, but how are you going to get there?"

"I'll jump in a cab. I forgot about the appointment, otherwise I would have taken my car this morning instead of riding with you. I'll meet you at home tonight," she said as she gently kissed him goodbye.

"Alright. Is everything okay?" he inquired.

"Yeah, honey, it's just a routine check up, that's all. I'll call you later."

"Alright. I love you, Denise."

"Love you, too, babe. I'll deal with you when I get home, Miss," she snapped at Katrina without looking at her.

"Let's go, Pumpkin," Corey said as he opened the passenger side of his car. "I think it's time for us to have a little father-daughter conversation. Get in."

Corey slammed the door and began to walk around to the other side of the car. Suddenly, he heard a familiar voice calling him from across the street. He looked and caught glimpse of a man wearing an Italian suit and toting a briefcase attempting to flag him down.

"C! C-Money!" he shouted as he dodged traffic and slowly jogged across the street.

"Who the...I don't fuckin' believe it," Corey softly said as he squinted at the man who approached him. "Gary?"

"C!" Gary shouted as he embraced Corey. "Long time no see, man."

161

Corey was absolutely flabbergasted. This couldn't have been the same man he knew over a decade ago. The man who just grabbed him and held him so tight that he could barely breathe was at least fifty pounds heavier than the man whose last words to him were, "I think I'm gonna go to one of those twelve-step programs and try to change my life around."

"W-What's up, Gary? I don't believe it. Is it really you?"

"Yeah, man, it's me alright," he proudly replied as he loosened his grapple from Corey's back. He took a step back to give Corey a better view. "Well, what do you think?" he asked.

"You've got to be fucking kidding me! Shit, how've you been, Gary?" Corey shouted before trying to squeeze the life out of him. "You look totally different. It's obvious that you've let the drugs go, that's for sure. What's goin' on?"

"Well, I did exactly what I promised I would. I decided to enter a program. From there, I knew the best thing for me to do was to get as far away from here as possible. You know, out of sight, out of mind. I moved out west, applied at one of those job placement training programs, got accepted, and passed at the top of my class. That sort of proved something to me. That I could become successful if I just put my mind to it. I later applied for financial aid at a local community college, received a Bachelors in education, and I've been teaching for the past two years. I recently decided to come home and return my blessings by teaching the children of those that I've harmed in the past."

"Whoa, I am thoroughly impressed. I know you're probably tired of hearing me say this, Gary, but I don't believe it," Corey said as he began to laugh. "I must say, though, I do commend you. So what brings you on this side of town?"

"Oh, I'm negotiating my contract at this high school today. And you?"

"I just had a meeting with my daughter and her vice-principal regarding her behavior."

"Who are you talking about? The only daughter I recall is Pumpkin, and I know you're not talking about her."

Corey didn't respond. Instead, he peeked through the rear window of his car and commenced to pound on the trunk. After catching her attention, he motioned Katrina to exit the car.

"Come over here a minute," he commanded as she stepped out of the vehicle. "I want to see if you remember someone."

Katrina stepped out of the car and walked toward her father. Gary displayed an astonished expression as she drew closer to him. He watched as a young lady, whose attire consisted of baggy jeans, a black hooded sweatshirt, black knitted hat, and a pair of construction work boots, approached him. The pants sagged approximately three inches below her waist. There was no way this could be the same sweet little girl he remembered playing in the park.

"Do you remember this man, Pumpkin?" Corey asked.

"No, why? Should I?"

"Hello, Pumpkin. I know you don't remember me. My name is Gary. I used to live around here years ago. Wow, I haven't seen you since you were this high," he giggled as he positioned his hand beside his knee cap.

"Yeah, I remember you," she casually replied. "You used to be a crack-head, right?" she sarcastically added.

"Katrina!" Corey interjected. "Damn, do you have

163

any respect?  Get your ass back in the damn car before I finish what your mother started," he snapped.  "Excuse her behavior, Gary.  This is what I've been dealing with for the past couple of years.  The only solution I've come up with is execution by firing squad," he jokingly stated.

"What grade is she in?"

"I believe the eleventh."

"The position I applied for deals with juniors and seniors.  I plan on working as the school's social worker.  There's a possibility that I may end up working with her in one way or another.  I can definitely request to have her placed on my list as one of my cases.  Why don't you give me a crack at it?  It's the best I can do to make up for what I tried to do to her mother years ago.  I'm not saying that it'll work, but I think it's worth a try."

"Wow, I really appreciate that, Gary.  My next step was to break my foot off in her ass and drop her off at a foster home with it still there."

"No, not just yet, Corey.  Listen, I've gotta get going.  My meeting starts in about five minutes," he said as he looked at his watch.  "Here, take my card and give me a call tomorrow.  Maybe we can grab dinner or something.  You know, reminisce."  He gave Corey a business card, smiled, and began walking toward the high school.

"Alright, Gary, it was great seeing you, man.  I'll definitely call you," Corey yelled as he opened his car door.

# CHAPTER
# 19

"Hey, Rich, you have to get those pallets stacked a little better than that!" Corey shouted from his office window to one of his foremen.

"Gotcha, boss," he replied. "Somebody get me a forklift over here and straighten out this disaster," Richard yelled.

As Corey slid his office window closed, Roman entered. "What's up, Corey?" he said. His greeting seemed to be more courteous than genuine.

"Hey, Rome, haven't seen you in a minute. What's going on?"

"Nothin' much. Been really busy, that's all," he replied as he pulled open a file drawer and began thumbing through folders.

Corey noticed Roman never gave him any eye contact. This wasn't new to Corey. Ever since his one night stand with Kimberly a year and a half ago, Roman's attitude towards Corey became pretty shady.

"Hey, listen…" Before Corey could finish his sentence, his cell phone began to ring. As he reached to answer it, Roman left the office without a word. "Hello? Hey, D, how's everything? Yeah, I should be home on time. Why? Really? A special dinner? What's the occasion? What? No children! I'll definitely be there. Alright, I'll see you then. Love you."

Corey placed his cell phone back on his belt and

began contemplating as to why Denise was suddenly in such a romantic mood. *"Oh my God,"* he thought to himself, *"she must be pregnant!"*

Corey impatiently anticipated leaving work to rendezvous with his wife for their "special" evening together. He hoped their conversation would pertain to the possible arrival of a new addition to their family. Corey knew they couldn't afford another child at the moment, but he felt having one might rekindle that spark which had been missing for some time. He and Denise decided after Malcolm they'd begin saving and searching for a new home in a better neighborhood, since the one they lived in at the moment was slowly becoming surrounded by the negativity they escaped from their previous home. That would be easier said than done, especially since they just discovered their daughter was the root of the majority of that negativity.

It was five o'clock and Corey quickly snatched his coat from a hook that was positioned behind his door. He raced across the dock and headed for the exit ramp to his car. *"Maybe I should grab some flowers before going home,"* he thought to himself.

Corey arrived home and, just as Denise promised, the children were not home. The aroma of a warm Italian dinner lingered in the hallway. He slowly walked past his dining room and caught glimpse of two candles flickering on the dining table. In a corner of the room, the silhouette of a beautifully shaped woman gently danced upon an adjacent wall.

"Hey, baby," a soft, seductive voice whispered. Although he could not see her, the sexiness of her voice seized his body and reeled it into the dining area.

Corey stepped into the dim room and immediately felt someone slide behind him and gently tease his eardrum.

"I'll take these, thank you," she softly said as she took a vase filled with a dozen white roses from his hands. "Close your eyes," her voice commanded.

Corey obeyed, and a silk scarf was placed over his eyes. The velvety sensation on his face caused goose pimples to rise over his body. His hand was grabbed and gently tugged.

"Follow me," she whispered. The sound almost caused the pimples to burst.

"Sit, please," she requested as she guided his body into a chair.

Corey sat down and the scarf was slowly removed from his eyes. To his delight, a steaming plate of lasagna sat in front of him. A bowl of seasoned fresh greens, tomato, cucumbers, and carrots was positioned beside it.

"Enjoy, my love," she said as she walked alongside the table and sat at its other end.

"Wow, Denise, this looks great," he said as he stared at his meal. He lifted his head and smiled at her. "What's the occasion?" he asked.

"Just eat your meal, sweetheart. We'll talk in a minute."

"Okay," he responded.

Corey scooped the last of his meal and wiped his mouth with a napkin. He looked at Denise, who sat quietly and patiently after finishing her meal, and asked, "Well, you wanna tell me what the occasion is?"

She smiled for a few seconds before responding. "It's a celebration."

"A celebration of what?" He then thought to himself, *"She never acted like this when she told me she was pregnant with the other kids."*

"A celebration of life, Corey, our life," she answered as her eyes filled with tears.

"W-What's wrong, Denise? You're scaring me," he said as he stood from his seat and began walking towards her.

"I took time today to reflect on everything we've been through, and I suddenly became terribly overwhelmed with joy. I realized more than ever that you and the children are my life. And, if I was reincarnated a thousand times, I would choose you over and over again."

Corey sat beside her and took her hand into his.

"I went to the doctor today," she continued.

"And?" Corey said as he attempted to restrain himself from smiling.

Her lower lip began to quiver. "I have breast cancer, Corey. It's too far gone. They have to be removed."

Corey stared at Denise and remained speechless. She began to realize he wasn't looking *at* her, but *past* her. The grip he had on her hand began to loosen, and his eyes became misty. Within those few seconds, at least a thousand questions must have entered and left his mind. How, why, will I lose her, can I get through this and how will I tell the kids, to name a few.

"Corey," Denise looked into her husband's eyes, confused as to what she should say next. "Corey, say something, please."

"I... I-I'm okay," he responded as he tried to redirect his thoughts back to what was taking place. He could feel his soul fluctuate between being courageous and falling into utter depression. His mind told him to console his wife, let her know he'd be there for her and that everything would be all right. His body, on the other hand, tingled and became limp. He felt as if he was falling into a never-ending abyss that he would not be able to climb out from.

"Corey, I'm okay, honey. I'm not afraid," she said, trying to reassure him as she grabbed his hand.

Mentioning the word "afraid" was all Corey needed to hear for his body to break down.

"*I'm* afraid, Denise," he sobbed as he fell to his knees and collapsed onto her lap. "I can't do this. Why you, huh? You don't deserve this!" His body tensed and became still. He wasn't breathing or moving anymore, just holding her tightly. Suddenly, he burst into a rage of tears. The pain he experienced from crying caused his back to arch as he desperately gasped for air.

Denise silently held his head in her hands. She slowly stroked the back of his head as tears quietly streamed down her face. The strange thing was she *wasn't* afraid. She wasn't crying because of her situation, but because she'd never seen her husband hurt this much. For as long as she could remember, Corey had always been strong. He didn't cry for either of his parents and shed only a few tears over the loss of his grandmother. She thought he would lose control of his emotions over what happened to Curtis, but as usual, he kept his composure. Now, for the first time, he was fragile. There were no signs of courage or strength and he had no motivational speeches to give. He just wept, motionless, slipping further and further into his abyss. And Denise didn't know how to bring him back to her. They sat and held each other until they fell asleep.

"Corey, honey, wake up," Denise whispered in his ear, oblivious as to how they ended up *under* the dining room table. "Wake up, baby."

"I'm awake," he responded as he rolled over to face her. "How are you feeling?"

"I'm fine, and you?"

"Exhausted. I didn't sleep all night. I remember helping you onto the carpet while you were sleep, but don't ask me how we wound up under this table," he said with a smile. "Guess I did doze off for a minute, huh?" he laughed.

"Hungry?" she asked.

"Not really. If *you* are, I'll make something for you," he responded. "Why don't you run upstairs and climb in the bed. Give me a few minutes and I'll be up with something to eat, okay?"

"Corey, you don't have to. I…"

"No, Denise, you've done this for years, and now it's obvious that it's my turn to step up to the plate," he said as he crawled from under their table. He leaned forward and offered his hand to her. "C'mon upstairs, Denise. I got this."

Denise stood in front of Corey and stared into his red, swollen eyes as she placed her arms over his shoulders. "Are you okay? I've never seen you like that before. I didn't know what to say to you last night."

"I'm better. It just took some time for everything to settle in, that's all. Years of pain, you know? I'm here for you and will be through this whole ordeal. I don't know what happened last night. That wasn't like me at all."

"No, that *was* like you, Corey. You finally showed me that you're a man. You cried. You never cry. You always shed a tear or two, then regain your composure. I don't know who told you real men don't cry, but they lied to you. You've always held everything in. Yes, Corey, you are strong. I know that. And through thick and thin, you've held this family together. But everyone breaks down, sweetheart."

"No, Denise, someone lied to *you*. Last night I realized you've always been my strength. *You* held this family together. *You* have always been its backbone. The children and I derived our strengths from *you*. When you told me your condition, I didn't know where to get my strength from. That's why I broke down the way I did. But I *am* going to get us through this. I *am* going to take control of this family and be the man that you need me to be. Now, on that note, go upstairs and wait for me to bring you something to eat."

She smiled for a moment. "I will, Corey. Just let me say one thing to you."

"What?" he asked.

"Don't find strength in me. Find strength in God," she said before gently kissing him on the cheek and turning away.

He watched as she left the dining room. "When is your surgery?" he inquired.

"Next Thursday morning," she answered as she ascended the stairs and disappeared into the bedroom.

# CHAPTER 20

"*D*enise, let's go!" Corey shouted. "You're running late. What are you doing?" he asked.

"I'm coming, Corey. Grab my bag, and I'll meet you at the car."

"Alright, just hurry up. You're supposed to be at the hospital by ten o'clock and it's already 9:45. I don't drive a Ferrari, you know," he rushed as he picked up her suitcase and walked through the door.

"*Thank you again, Lord, for everything you've given to me and my family. Please allow me to come through this surgery successfully so that I may return to my family. Amen.*" Denise stood from the edge of her bed, grabbed her coat, and left her bedroom.

"How do you feel?" Corey asked as he backed out of their driveway.

"Nervous," she responded. "You?"

"Nervous. I know everything's gonna be alright, but still, I can't help feeling this way. I still haven't figured out a way to tell the children yet. I think Katrina will be fine, but I don't think Kareem is going to handle it too well. Malcolm is still too young to understand."

"I've been thinking about the same thing. Just tell them that I had an emergency meeting out of town. When I return, we'll discuss everything as a family, okay?"

"Okay."

Corey escorted his wife into the hospital and toward the elevators. "What floor, honey?"

"Fourth," she replied.

As they exited the elevator, she recognized a familiar face approaching her. "Hello, Denise."

"Oh my God, Dr. Tisdale, how've you been?"

"I'm fine," he said as he hugged her. "I was speaking with one of my colleagues yesterday when he mentioned he had to perform a mastectomy this morning. He told me that his patient had given birth here on more than one occasion. I asked him the patient's name and became stunned when he mentioned you. Why wasn't I or your mother informed?"

"I didn't want to let her know until after the surgery, and I knew if I told you, you would have told her."

"You're wrong, Denise. There *is* that little thing called confidentiality, you know. Anyway, I told your doctor that your mother was very dear to me and he assured me that he'd take special care of you."

"That's very kind of you, Dr. Tisdale. I…"

"That's another thing," he interjected. "I've been seeing your mother for almost four years now and I'd appreciate it if you would just call me David."

"Well, David, since it's been that long, how about if I just called you Dad? I know how serious you and my mother are, and I'm old enough to know that you're not trying to replace my father. I do respect and love you for the joy you've given to my mother, and I would prefer to refer to you as Dad than call you by your first name, if that's all right with you."

He paused for a moment. "I'd like that a lot, Denise. You know I don't have any children of my own. My ex-wife, God rest her soul, was barren, so I've never been able to experience the pleasure of someone calling me by that name. I am truly honored and I promise to try to treat you as a daughter. Now, let's get ready to get this over with. Follow me," he said as he grabbed her hand and led her to the changing room.

Corey watched as an orderly pushed Denise on a gurney toward the operating room. He raised his hand to his mouth and blew a kiss at her as the gurney slammed into the double doors of the room, and caught a distant glimpse of her blowing a kiss back as the doors closed.

"Denise...Denise, wake up, dear."

Denise's eyelids fluttered as she tried to focus on the smiling image that leaned over her.

"Can you hear me?" the nurse asked.

"Where am I?" Denise questioned.

"In a recovery room. You've just had surgery, dear. How do you feel?"

"Where's my husband?"

"He's outside. I'll bring him in for you."

"I'm so thirsty. Can you bring me something to drink, please?"

"Sure thing, dear."

Moments after the nurse left the room, Corey entered with a bouquet of flowers and balloons.

"Hey, baby," he said as he kissed her forehead. "How do you feel?"

"Sore," she replied.

"Your doctor informed me that the surgery was a success and that you should be outta here within the next day or two depending on how quickly you recover."

"What time is it?"

Corey looked at his watch. "Six-thirty."

"In the morning?" she inquired in a raspy voice.

"No," he replied with a smile, "the evening. Wow, how long did you think you were under?"

"I have no idea, Corey. I'm experiencing serious time distortions at the moment. You stayed here all day?"

"Where else am I supposed to be? I called home and spoke with Katrina. She said everything was fine. She asked where we were and I told her what you told me to tell her. I told her I was running a little late and that I needed her to cook something for dinner, you know hotdogs or something."

"Oh God, she's gonna burn down the house," she giggled.

"Hey, you'd better stop laughing before you crack those dry ass lips. Got any lip balm?"

"Stop making fun of me, Corey," she said as she raised her sheet over her face. "I have some Vaseline in my bag. Will you hand it to me, please?"

"No problem, D. Hope you got a few mints in here, as well. Smells like you've been sleeping for over a year."

"Corey…"

"I'm just trying to make you laugh, Denise, and raise your spirits a little."

"How do I look, Corey?" The expression on her face suddenly became very serious.

"As beautiful as the first day I laid eyes on you," he replied.

"Here's your water, dear," the nurse said as she pushed a cart into the recovery room. "I also brought a pitcher of ice chips to help ease the cottonmouth sensation you're experiencing. You're going to remain in this room for a few hours before someone comes to transfer you to your room, so get comfortable. Mr. Lambert, I know you want to stay and watch over your wife, but she needs to rest. And, looking at your eyes, you could use a little sleep yourself."

"Actually, I was just leaving," he informed her. "Denise, I'll be back tomorrow evening. I've got a little catching up to do at work before I come to the hospital. Make sure you call me if you need anything, alright?"

"I will, honey. Give me some love."

Corey hesitantly leaned over and kissed Denise on her cheek.

"What? Not on the lips, Corey?" she asked.

"Maybe tomorrow," he said before smiling and kissing her on the forehead, "after the Vaseline kicks in."

"Oh, forget you." She tapped him on his hand. "You're so bad."

"I know. That's why you love me," he said as he left the room. "Goodnight, sweetheart."

"Goodnight, Corey."

# CHAPTER
# 21

"Hey, Mom, what happened to you?" Katrina asked as she held the front door open for her parents.

"I'll tell you guys all about it as soon as I get settled in. Kareem, can you bring my things in for me? Don't forget my flowers. Where's Malcolm?"

"He's upstairs taking a nap," Katrina replied.

"Wow, who cleaned the house?" Denise said as she slowly walked into the living room.

"Daddy and I did. Well, Kareem helped a little."

"I heard you, Pumpkin," Kareem said as he placed his mother's flowers on the coffee table. "What you meant to say is Daddy and Kareem cleaned it."

"Yeah, whatever. I was too busy looking after Malcolm."

"If that's what you want to call it. Mommy, what happened to you? You don't look so well."

"Sit down for a minute, guys. There's something we need to talk about. Corey, would you mind making me a cup of tea, please?"

"No problem, D. You need anything else?"

"No, that's it for now. Thanks."

"Listen, I know both of you are wondering what's going on. Your mother has been in the hospital for the past two days."

"For what?" Kareem asked.

"I had to have a surgical procedure known as a mastectomy performed. In other words, I had to have my breasts removed."

"Why?" Katrina asked as her eyes filled with tears.

"I had breast cancer, Pumpkin."

"How?" Kareem asked. "You don't even smoke."

"Smoking has nothing to do with it, baby. There are different forms of cancer and many ways of getting it. The problem is, I found out about mine too late. So my breast had to be taken off."

"Are you all right now?" Kareem asked as he sat next to his mother and held her hand.

"Yes, I just need to take it easy and try to recover over the next couple of weeks."

"Well, as long as you're all right, I'll be all right," he told her.

"Here's your tea, honey. Katrina, go and find the number to the pizzeria. It looks like we'll be hoofing it for the next few days."

"By the time Mommy gets better, we'll have burgers, pizza, and oodles of noodles coming out of our ears," Kareem said as he placed a pillow behind his mother's head.

"I'm going upstairs, Mom. Do you need anything?" Katrina asked.

"No, Pumpkin. Are you okay?"

"I'll be fine," she responded as she walked upstairs to her room.

"Did you order dinner, Pumpkin?" Corey shouted out after a couple minutes of her being upstairs.

"Yeah," she answered.

"C'mon, Denise, let me take you upstairs."

As he helped Denise from the couch, it reminded him of her mother. "Did you call Momma Di yet?"

"Not yet, Corey," she replied.

"How about Tina?"

"No."

"Do you want me to contact them for you?"

"Yes, but tell them not to come by until tomorrow. You know how they are. They'll be knocking down the front door seconds after you hang the phone up with them. I need to rest first before I'm bombarded with TLC."

"Well, in that case, I think it'd be better if I just wait until morning to call them. You know once I tell them what's goin' on, nothing will keep them away from you. Anyway, tomorrow's Sunday and your mother never misses church, so that might assist us in delaying her visit. I doubt very seriously that she'd shorten her *Sabbath*, even for you."

"You're so silly, Corey. Just help me up the stairs and into bed before I tell my mother what you said about her."

"Hi, Momma Di," Corey said as he opened the door. "Hey, Tina."

"Hello, son. Where's my baby?" she said as she quickly brushed past him.

"She's in the living room, Momma."

Tina walked up to Corey, grabbed the front of his shirt, and pulled him to her. "How could you keep this from me, Corey?" she mumbled. "You were supposed to be my brother!"

"It was her request, Tina, I swear," he whispered. "Oh, hello, Dr. Tisdale. I didn't expect you here."

"I felt it was my obligation," he replied.

For a moment, Corey was stumped by the remark the doctor made. But he looked at Diana as she walked into the living room and began to put two and two together.

"So how have things been with you and Momma Di?" he inquired as he took the doctor's coat and reached into the closet for a hanger.

"Wonderful, thanks for asking. She is the most beautiful woman I've ever had the pleasure of meeting, not only physically, but spiritually as well. Between you and me, I've been contemplating proposing to her. She is the woman that I hope to leave this earth married to."

"Whoa! Are you serious?"

"Absolutely," he confirmed.

"Well, let me congratulate you in advance. Shoot, I say go for it if she makes you that happy. I know her daughter does for me every single day. I'm just sorry it took so long for me to realize it," he said, glancing towards the living room.

"What do you mean?"

"Uh, nothing. You want a beer or something?"

"No. Your mother-in-law would kill me if she knew that I indulged in alcohol on a Sunday. Maybe some scotch if you have any," he smiled.

"That's more like it. You had me worried for a minute, Doc."

"Please, call me David."

"Okay, David, you had me worried. C'mon, the dining room's this way."

"Honey, why didn't you tell me what was going on?" Denise's mother asked.

"I didn't want you to worry, so I decided not to let you know until after the surgery."

"What about me?" Tina asked.

"I knew you'd tell Momma. You always do."

"This is different, Denise. That was so selfish of you."

"Listen, Tina, I know you still feel compelled to take care of me, but I have Corey now. You're still my big sister and you know I love you with all of my heart, but I have a family here that comes first and there are certain things we have to deal with alone before I inform everyone else. What you can do, though, is keep an eye out for Jackie and Michelle for me. They both need you to guide them, and they feel the same way about you as I do."

"Well, since you've mentioned them, I've been sort of 'selfish' myself."

"What are you talking about, Tina?"

"I found out some disheartening news and I didn't call to let you know about it."

"What news?"

"Jackie called me yesterday. Michelle's in the hospital."

"For what?" Denise asked.

"Well, she wasn't feeling well, so she went to the emergency room. She was told she had pneumonia, and after the doctors ran a few tests on her, they found she had full blown AIDS."

"Oh my Lord," Diana interjected. "I knew that something was going to happen to that young girl."

"Are you serious?" Denise said, her hands trembling over her mouth. "Please tell me that you're not sure, Tina."

"We're sure, sis. Jackie and I were trying to figure out how to tell you. We knew you'd take it pretty hard. I know this is bad timing, but I didn't know when else to tell you. I felt if I waited any longer…it would have been too late." Tina placed her head in her hands and burst into tears.

"How did she get it?" Denise inquired.

"Her boyfriend. That nigga gave it to her," she said as she became more emotional.

"Watch that N-word, Tina," Diana interrupted.

"I'm sorry, Momma, but that's what he was!" she shouted. "A forty ounce drinking, weed smoking, unemployed nigger who took my friend from me," she cried as she stood up and ran from the living room.

"Tina!" Denise shouted.

"Let her go and vent, honey," her mother requested.

"Momma, why?" she asked as she began to weep. "Why is this happening?"

"I've been trying to tell you all your life, Denise, what you do will always come back on you. That young girl chose the life she led and she wasn't stupid. She knew the dangers of the streets. God sets the stage for us, but the choices we make dictate the outcome. That's not to say if you live a clean and wholesome life you'll live to be a hundred years old, because your due date is your due date. But we have to realize that if you smoke, you may get cancer. If you drink, you may develop cirrhosis of the liver, and if you play with God's laws, you WILL get burned."

"So what about me, Momma? What did I do to deserve this?" she said as she placed her hands over her chest.

"That was written for you, my child. It had nothing to do with the life you led or the choices you made. Your test is in the way you react to your situation."

"What the hell is going on in here?" Corey said as he entered the dining room. "Ooh, I'm sorry, Momma Di. What's going on?" he asked as he looked at Denise.

"Michelle's in the hospital, Corey."

"Oh yeah? What's her problem? There's no breast for her to get cancer in, so what is it? Oh, wait a minute... alcoholics anonymous. No, hold on...hygiene anonymous. Wait, I've got it..."

"Corey, she has AIDS!!"

"What! Are you serious?"

"Yes, Corey," she answered as she burst into tears.

"Oh my God, Denise, I'm sorry. I didn't know," he said as he sat beside her and pulled her into his arms. "How did you find out?"

"Tina just told me."

"Where is she?" he asked as he looked around the room.

"I don't know. She got up and left a few minutes ago. She might be on the porch. See if you can find her, Corey. She's taking this pretty hard."

"No problem," he said as he stood from the sofa. "I'll be right back."

As Corey left the living room, he bumped into Dr. Tisdale. "Where's your bathroom, Corey?" he asked.

"Down the hall and on your left," he responded in a rushed voice.

"Is everything all right, Corey?"

"Not really," he said as he continued toward the front door.

Corey opened the door and noticed Tina sitting on the banister staring into the sky.

"You okay, Tina?"

"I'll be fine. Thanks."

"You wanna talk?"

"Forget about me. How are you holding up?"

"Too much shit at one time, that's for sure."

183

"You couldn't be more right."

"I guess I'll make it through, though. Where's Jackie?"

"She said she'll be here later. She's been pretty depressed since yesterday, you know."

"Yeah, you guys have to stick together through this. I've never seen women that weren't related treat each other like sisters the way you guys do. That's a special friendship. I've been praying that Denise comes through this okay. She's my world, you know. I've been trying to be strong in her presence, but I crumble whenever I'm not with her. I don't know what I'd do without her. Anyway, you're gonna have to toughen up and be the big sister they need you to be right now, just as I have to be the man Denise needs me to be."

"Wow, who would have ever thought you and I would be having a civilized conversation, or even agree with each other?"

"Yeah, who woulda thought," he concurred.

They looked at each other momentarily. "Yuk!" they said in unison.

"Let's go inside, bro," she suggested.

"Alright, tree monster," he replied.

"Whatever," she said as she pushed him through the door.

As Corey and Tina entered the house, they saw Katrina coming downstairs toward them.

"Hey, Auntie. Dad, I need to get out for a minute. I hope that's not a problem."

"What time are you coming back?"

"Dad, it's Saturday."

"What's that supposed to mean?"

"Never mind. What time do you want me back?" she

casually inquired.

"Isn't your curfew at eleven?"

"Yes."

"Then be here at eleven."

"Where's Mommy?" she asked, her tone the same.

"In the living room."

Katrina immediately turned and headed for the living room. "Hi, Grandma!" she shouted as she rushed to hug her.

"My Lord, child, what have you been eating, furniture?! You're so big."

"No, Grandma, I like to work out."

"Work out what?! I know you're not talking about lifting any weights? What's wrong with you, girl?"

"It's rough out here, Grandma. I've gotta be strong enough to protect myself."

"Well, if you weren't 'out here', you wouldn't need to protect yourself, now would you? Where are you going now?"

"To meet some of my friends at the arcade."

"The ar-who?" she asked.

"The arcade, Grandma. It's where teenagers meet to play video games and hang out."

"Don't you think your mother may need you here, child?"

"It's all right, Momma," Denise interrupted. "Katrina, you know your curfew. Respect it."

"I know, Mom. See ya, Grandma."

Corey, Tina, and Doctor Tisdale entered the living room as Katrina left. "Does anyone need anything?" Corey asked.

"No, thank you," they all replied.

"So what's next?"

"We prepare for the worst, Corey," Diana answered. "We prepare for the worst."

# CHAPTER 22

# Katrina:
# 3-17-98

"All rise," the bailiff commanded. "The Honorable Judge Johnson presiding."

"Please, be seated," the Judge requested as he took his seat. "I hope everyone enjoyed their lunch break. Now, let's see if we can finish up early so that we can get home. Well, some of us anyway. Who do I have next?"

"Your Honor, the state calls Katrina Lambert. Katrina is being represented by court appointed attorney, William Pryce."

"How does your client plea, Council?" the judge asked.

"My client would like to enter a plea of guilty with an explanation, your Honor."

"Continue…wait a second. Why does this name seem so familiar?" he queried as he stared at a folder. "Lambert… Lambert…I know that name." He took off his reading glasses to catch a better glimpse of who stood before him. "Ah, yes, now I remember. I thought I told you I didn't want to see you in my courtroom again, Miss. What's your excuse this time?"

"Sir, I was at the wrong place at the wrong time," she replied.

"Really? Would you like to explain how you expect me to change a charge from aggravated assault to 'the wrong place at the wrong time'?"

"I wasn't involved, sir. Some other girls jumped her. I just happened to be walking out of the store when the police arrived."

At this point, not only did the judge know she was lying, the whole courtroom knew it, as well. It may have been the aggressive posture she displayed while facing the judge. Or maybe it was the unmoved expression she carried on her face. Whatever it was, it wasn't working in her favor.

Corey and Denise sat and watched as their eldest daughter's fate sat in the palms of a man whose face looked as if it were chiseled by a professional sculptor. This man had absolutely no facial expressions. His face remained fixed at all times, as if it belonged in the center of a promissory note. If anyone took notice, they would have realized Corey and Denise shared the same expression. By this time, they were ready to give up. If not, they knew one of them was probably destined to have a stroke or heart attack. At this point, whatever decision the judge rendered was fine with them.

"Your Honor," Mr. Pryce interceded.

"Yes, Council?"

"I have a young man here today who is willing to take this young lady under his wing as a mentor, and hopefully, turn her life around."

"And who might that be?"

"His name is Gary Simmons, your Honor. He's a social worker at the high school and claims to have known my client for many years." Gary stood up and walked over to the public defender to give the judge a better look at him.

"Well, today seems to be a day of *repetitive* déjà vu. You *also* look like someone I told never to enter my courtroom again. You can't be that man, though. I must have seen him at least ten or twelve times in this court many years ago. I remember telling him that he'd better find a good rehabilitation program to enter because if I ever saw him again, I'd sentence him to ten years in prison. Now, although you're much larger than the person I'm speaking of, that wouldn't have been you, now would it?"

Gary remained silent, knowing the judge wasn't looking for a reply. Anyone who met Gary even once in their lifetime would have had a hard time forgetting him. It was obvious Judge Johnson remembered him, but if this was the new man he became, he couldn't resist giving him the opportunity for redemption.

"Council, will you and Mr. Simmons please approach the bench?"

"Yes, your Honor," they replied in unison.

"Mr. Simmons, I'd like to first say that I am very proud of what you've become," he whispered, "and I am going to give you the opportunity to hopefully change this young lady. I will, however, be placing her on house arrest for the next six months, during which she will report to you on a weekly basis for a ninety minute counseling session. This counseling session will be used at your discretion. In other words, whether you choose to have her wash chalkboards, empty trash, or write essays is strictly up to you. After the six month period, your client must report back to my courtroom, Mr. Pryce, for my personal evaluation. If I am satisfied with her progress, I will terminate her probation. If not, she will be sentenced to another six months at The Center for Juvenile Girls. And you, Mr. Simmons, will once again be banned from my courtroom. Do we have an understanding?"

"Yes, your Honor," they replied.

"Good. Then inform your client of my decision, Mr. Pryce."

"Thank you, your Honor," he said as he returned to Katrina and escorted her and her parents from the courtroom. As they left the courtroom and entered the hallway, the public defender explained the judge's decision.

"What!" Katrina shrieked. "He might as well lock me up! An ankle bracelet? Is he crazy?!"

"Katrina, lower your voice," Denise snapped as she grabbed Katrina's arm and began to squeeze it tightly.

"Ow, Mom, alright," she whispered.

"Katrina, darling, you do realize that if you are unsatisfied with the judge's verdict, you could always reenter the courtroom and request jail time instead," Corey sarcastically implied.

"Corey!" Denise said, shocked at her husband's statement.

"It would definitely make things easier on your mother and me if you weren't at home. That way, we wouldn't have to worry about taking care of you anymore and it would be one less mouth we would have to feed," he added as he turned and began to walk away from her. "We could leave all of that up to the penile system."

As Corey walked down the hall, he could hear Katrina crying, "Mommy, he doesn't love me anymore."

"Yes, he does, Pumpkin. He's just disappointed in you," she consoled.

Corey didn't mean what he said to her. He just hoped what was said would strike a nerve. This game he and Denise were playing was a classical scene from "good parent, bad parent". It's a psychological game parents sometimes play on their children to possibly dupe them into changing their behavior. Usually, the parent closest in relationship to the child pretends to dislike him/her because of the behavior they've been displaying. When, in fact, it is the behavior that is disliked and not the child. The parent whose rapport with the child is less than that of the supposedly "disappointed" parent consoles the child, thereby increasing their relationship. During this phase, the child becomes bent on reestablishing his/her relationship with the other parent by attempting to change the unexceptional behavior. No matter how you look at it, it's always a win-win situation for both parents.

"Mommy?"

"Yes, Pumpkin?"

"After this is over with, I'm going to try and change my ways. I've been thinking a lot lately about my life and where I'm going with it. Malcolm told me I was his best friend the other day and that he wants to be like me when he grows up. He doesn't even know what I am or all the dirt I've done. It's crazy to think that I, of all people, have someone who looks up to me, not because he fears me, but because he loves me. Mommy, I've done so many things in my life to hurt people...things you can't even imagine."

"Do you want to talk about it?"

"No. I just don't want to live that life anymore, and I don't know how to get out. Mom, can I ask you a question?"

"Sure, what is it, Pumpkin?"

"Am I what you expected me to be?"

"Well," she paused, "to tell the truth, I always knew you'd be a piece of work, girl. I didn't think it would almost land you in prison, but go figure. Actually, you were always very bright and outgoing. Yes, I'm surprised you used your charisma and charm for evil instead of good, but you're still young. The good thing is I hear that you've got quite some following in the streets and you're still young. You can change your life and those around you at anytime. Just remember, the length of time it took you to get to this point may be the same length of time for you to change it. I believe in you, Pumpkin, and always have. You just need to believe the same."

"I love you, Mom, and I'm gonna change. I promise," she said as she hugged her mother.

"I love you, too, Pumpkin. Now, let's catch up with your father before we're both on the bus."

# CHAPTER
# 23

"So Brian, you have two days to turn in that report to me. If I think it's satisfactory, I agree to speak with Mrs. Prescott and see if we can get your after-school detention program terminated. Agreed?"

"Yes, Mr. Simmons, thanks. You know, Mr. Simmons, I think you're probably the best social worker this school's ever had."

"I appreciate that, Brian. Alright, hurry up and get to class."

As Brian exited the office, Katrina squeezed through the doorway to enter. When Brian realized whose path he'd been obstructing, he immediately jumped back and attempted to hold the door for her.

"M-My bad, Pumpkin," he stuttered.

"Just get the fuck outta my way, geek ass," she mumbled as she stepped past him.

"Miss Lambert, please tell me that you didn't just disrespect my office," Gary stated.

"Uh, no, sir, I didn't."

"Good. Then sit your behind down in that chair and prepare for your session," he said as he pointed to a chair positioned on the other side of his desk. "And take out a pencil and notebook. You *do* have a pencil and notebook, don't you?"

Katrina stared at Gary as if he were speaking another language. "No, I don't."

"Okay then, from now on you will come to your sessions prepared. Is that clear?"

"Yes, sir."

"And stop with the 'sir' routine. This isn't boot camp. Refer to me as Mr. Simmons. Has your father told you anything about me since he introduced us?"

"No."

"Well, let me explain why I decided to work with you. About ten years ago, your father and I witnessed one of our best friends get murdered."

"You mean Curtis?"

"Oh, you remember him?"

"Yeah, about as much as I remember you," she sarcastically stated.

"Anyway, I was sitting so close to him when it happened, blood splattered on my face after the bullet hit him. Your father and I never really got along before that incident took place. I *was* a crack-head at the time, just as you recalled. Don't misunderstand me, though. He and I were friends *before* I started doing drugs. One day, I tried to snatch your mother's pocketbook from her shoulder, and I think the only reason your father didn't try to kill me was because he felt sorry for me and the condition I was always in. He wasn't the only one who was disappointed with me. I hurt a lot of people when I was in the streets, just as I'm sure you have. Curtis was a true friend and a brother to me. I believe the only reason he hung out with me was because he knew I was always too high to take care of myself. At any rate, his murder changed me. Sometimes I feel as if I could have prevented it if I wasn't so high. Then again, maybe it was just his time to go."

"Excuse me, Mr. Simmons," she interrupted. "No

disrespect, but you wanna tell me what all of this has to do with me?"

"First, let me ask you one question. Do you smoke marijuana?"

"Marijuana?" she repeated, as if she'd never heard the word before.

"Yes, marijuana, reefer, weed, grass, pot, hydro, chocolate, whatever you want to call it. Just answer the question."

"Since you want me to be honest, yeah, I smoke *goods* every once in a while."

"Good, because that's exactly how I started."

"Okay, I guess you're about to give me the 'gateway drug' speech now, right?"

"No. Actually, I'm just trying to make a point. You have an addiction, just as I did when I was younger."

"Mr. Simmons, I don't have an addiction," she responded in an offended tone.

"Let me finish. Your addiction *is* different from the one I had, but it's still an addiction."

"How you figure?" she asked.

"Your addiction to fame and power has corrupted you. And, on top of that, you're getting high, which only intensifies your desires. When you smoke, do you feel invincible?"

"Yeah, sometimes."

"Do you care about how others feel, or is it all about you and want you want?"

"Yeah, it's pretty much all about me. But you act like I get high by myself and do dirt by myself."

"No, I don't. The ones that get high with you are trying to fulfill their desires, also. The difference between them and you is, they're followers and you're a leader. How many friends do you have? And I mean true friends."

"One. My boy, big L."

"Is he part of your gang?"

"No. He runs the K.O.K., but he's locked up right now in juvey for conspiracy to murder."

"The K.O.K. I see that name spray painted a lot around the neighborhood. What does it stand for?"

"Oh, they're called the Knockout Kings. They're our brother gang. They get in a lot more trouble than we do because they get more felonies than us, but we're still respected for what we do."

"Are you listening to yourself?"

"What?" she asked with a dumbfounded expression.

"Is that what your life has come down to, competing to see who can get the most felonies?"

"No, I..."

"Listen, Katrina, the bottom line is, over the next few months I am going to teach you about self respect. See, self respect will not only sway you away from being involved with drugs, but it will also increase your respect for others. I'm not saying you're a drug addict, but trust me when I say that you're on your way. From now on, everyday will be a positive lesson. We're gonna see if we can get you away from that street mentality you seem to adore so much. Deal?"

"I guess," she answered.

"So, I'll see you tomorrow then?" he said as he stood and extended his hand.

"Yes, Mr. Simmons. Is that the end of our session?"

"Yes. I don't think it's necessary to keep you here for ninety minutes every time we see each other. As long as I get my point across and you continue to put forth an effort, then I believe a short meeting can be just as productive as a long one."

"Cool." Katrina shook his hand, turned, and left the office. As she walked out, she thought to herself, *"That nigga must be outta his mind if he thinks we're doing this shit every week."*

Katrina continued down the hall to class. Suddenly, she decided to make a detour. She turned left, headed for an exit sign that flickered above a pair of double doors, and quickly crept through them. She immediately scurried across a football field, ducked behind a pair of bleachers, reached into her pocket, and pulled out half of a blunt she had put out earlier that day. "Shit, I can stop smoking this whenever the fuck I feel like it," she told herself as she lit it.

As she slowly floated towards her castle in the sky, something caused her to momentarily grasp reality. She opened one of her eyes and caught glimpse of a group of girls walking toward her. She lifted her foot and quickly extinguished what was once an ordinary cigar. The group drew closer and Katrina began to recognize their faces. They were all part of her faction.

"What's going on?" Katrina asked her crew as she stepped from behind the bleachers. "What y'all doin' out here?"

"What's up, K.K.?" one of the girls said. "Don't even try it. We saw smoke. Where's the blunt?" she asked.

"It's not enough for everybody to hit, so I'm not gonna light it up right now," Katrina responded. "Who the fuck is this?" she asked as she stared at an unfamiliar face. "And why the hell is she in my presence?"

"Oh, this is Rhonda. She's a new prospect," another replied.

"Beat it, Rhonda," Katrina commanded. "And, René,

don't bring anymore prospects to me until they've been jumped in and made official. You hear me?"

"Yeah, K.K.," René answered. "You heard her. Beat it, bitch!" she yelled as she pushed Rhonda away from their group.

Katrina's name was changed to K.K. for two reasons: one, out of respect, and two, because she was involved in a homicide that took place when she and a group of females literally beat a teenaged girl to death. The murder was an accident. The group was attempting to initiate a new member into their gang by "jumping her in", when she suddenly took a violent blow to the temple. Ironically, it was Katrina who delivered the fatal blow that killed the girl. All of the girls who were involved knew it was Katrina who dropped the teen to her knees, and immediately dubbed her Killer Katrina, or K.K. for short. What they didn't know was that the body of the young girl, which lied motionless against the cold hardwood floor, would remain there until a group of young children, who were playing in the abandoned building, found her four days later. No one who witnessed the murder ever spoke of it to anyone. It became "their little secret". From that day forward, the youth in the neighborhood assumed Katrina was the founder of K.O.Q., but the dark enigma of the events which took place that day were the true reasons behind her monarchy.

Getting "jumped in" means an individual allows a group of people, male or female depending on the rules, to kick and pummel them for a designated time period. Once they've survived the time frame, they're considered one of the members of whichever organization they were "applying" for.

Katrina was two months away from her seventeenth

birthday, and her fighting and survival skills could have easily assisted her in surviving a life sentence in an adult, all male, correctional facility. What confused most people was, take away her size, Katrina was a very attractive young lady. If she ever decided to shed twenty or thirty pounds, she would have had no problem applying for an ad at any modeling agency, and actually get the job. Long beautiful hair, large, dark eyes and a flawless, ebony skin tone were just a few of her rare qualities. Take away the battle scars that embellished her face, and she would have put the Mona Lisa to shame.

"The rest of you should be somewhere recruiting instead of standing here trying to get a puff of my weed. René, you stay here with me. I need to talk to you for a minute."

"Y'all heard her. Go and get busy!" As the group of girls dispersed, René turned to face Katrina. "What's up, K.K.?" she asked.

"Nothing. I just need to ask you something, that's all. Listen, I'm thinking about leaving K.O.Q. I want you to finish what I started. Is that cool?"

"No, not really. Why you trying to bounce on us?" she asked.

"It's not that I'm trying to just bounce on you guys. Something happened to make me think about what I've been doing. The point is, outta everybody I roll with, I trust you the most. We've got a few years under our belt together and I know you. We've done some serious shit and I feel that you've always had my back, especially since L's been locked up. You've been my sister and you're the one I would want to take care of the rest of the girls."

"So, if I'm your sister, the least you can do is tell me why you wanna step down all of a sudden?"

"It's my little brother, Malcolm. He was kinda tellin'

me how much I meant to him and that he wanted to be like me when he got older. I don't want him doing all this fucked up shit we've been doin' all these years. I'm a fuckin' disgrace to my parents, and all I need is for him to turn out like me. That would just be something else that I ruined in my life. I'm beginning to feel like that King. You know, what's his name? Everything that I touch turns to shit." Katrina paused, pulled her blunt from her pocket, and began to light it. As she held the smoke inside of her lungs, she began to speak again while trying to inhibit her cough. "You heard about that motherfucker I've been seeing after school for counseling, right?"

"Yeah, Mr. Simmons or something," René responded as she took the blunt from Katrina. "I heard he was pretty cool," she said before inhaling.

"Whatever. He knows my parents. The nigga was sayin' some alright shit, though. He was sayin' something about self respect and respecting others. The self respect part flew right over my head, but the respecting others part made me think about Malcolm for some reason. Of all people, Malcolm looks up to me. I don't even talk to his little ass!" she said as she began laughing. "Why couldn't he look up to Kareem? He's the smart one."

René began to giggle at Katrina's statement and handed the blunt back to her. "Yeah, ain't he like some kinda nerd or something?"

"What the fuck is so funny?"

"No, I'm sayin', he is cute." René suddenly ceased her laughter.

"Yo, be serious for a minute. Do you think you can handle it or what?"

"Of course, but what about our '*blood in, blood out*'

rule?" René asked.

"I made that rule, so let me deal with it."

"I know, but rival gangs are going to think we're weak. That includes our brother clique."

"You sound like you wanna do me right here, sis. I would respect that if you tried to. It would show your loyalty to the family and its code."

"No, that's not what I was thinking. It's just no one has ever left before, not a captain, a general, no one. My loyalty is to the family, but it doesn't come anywhere near the loyalty I have to you."

"I hear you," Katrina said as she hugged René. "So will you do it?" she asked.

"I would do anything you asked me to, K.K." She looked at Katrina and extended her hand. They began offering their secretive handshakes to each other.

"I appreciate it. I'm about to get up outta here. I'll catch up with you later on."

"Don't you have to see Mr. Simmons this afternoon?"

"No, I had a session with him during my study hall period. I don't have to see him again until next week. The funny thing is that I'm kinda looking forward to seeing what the fuck he has to say."

Katrina turned and began to exit the field. If only she was able to see the look of deceit René wore upon her face as she watched her walk away.

# CHAPTER
# 24

"*Is* anybody home?" Katrina shouted as she entered her house.

"Yeah, me and Malcolm are upstairs," Kareem yelled from his bedroom.

Katrina walked past Malcolm and Kareem's room and noticed Malcolm was sitting alone, playing a video game. She felt this would be the perfect opportunity to commence with her so-called "mentoring program".

"Hey, Mal, what you doing?" she asked as she sat beside him.

Kareem lifted his head from a book he was reading. "What, you don't know how to knock anymore?" he asked.

"I know how to *knock* you the fu…" Katrina paused and remembered the mission she was on. "Never mind, we can go in my room if you need your privacy, Kareem."

"It's not that serious, Pumpkin. I'm actually glad you've finally decided to come *into* our room," Kareem said, smiling at her.

"Yeah, we're glad," Malcolm agreed. "I'm playing Ninja Fighters, II. You wanna battle me?"

"Yeah, why not? I got some skills. Move over, kid."

"You'll be calling me 'man' after I finish whippin' your behind, Pumpkin." Malcolm leaned forward and pressed the reset button on his game console.

"You wish. Just start the game."

As Katrina and Malcolm engaged in battle, Kareem sat silently and watched. He wondered what could have possibly happened to cause his sister to suddenly want to *be* a sister.

"Yeah!" Katrina shouted after obtaining another victory. "I told you I had skills. Kareem, is that the doorbell?" she asked without taking her eyes from the television.

"Its' obvious you two aren't gonna check to see if it is, so I might as well," he said as he left the bedroom. Seconds later, he yelled upstairs, "Katrina, it's for you!"

As Katrina made her way downstairs, she began to recognize the bluish grey suit worn by the man who stood on her front porch. It was the same one she had seen a few hours earlier. "May I help you, Mr. Simmons?" she asked as she stepped past her brother.

"Hello, Katrina. I won't take up much of your time. I stopped by for two reasons. First, to make sure you were home where you belong. And second, I forgot to give you this book. It's the autobiography of Malcolm X. Do you know of him?"

"Yeah, I heard of him before, but I don't know much about him. Ain't he the one who said something about 'by any means necessary'?"

"Well, you're right about that part. But is that all you know about him?" he asked.

"Yeah, that's about it," she replied.

"Good then. That's more reason for you to read it. It changed my life and I think it will change yours, especially after you read where he came from and the lifestyle he lived before going to prison. I'm giving you two weeks to finish it."

"Two weeks? Aw c'mon, Mr. Simmons," she whined

as she took the book from his hands.

"Listen, don't push it. I'm being merciful because I know you have a lot of other homework assignments that you have to complete, right?" He winked before turning to leave. "I'll see you in my office next week, and make sure you're in school tomorrow."

"See ya, Mr. Simmons," she replied in a depressed tone as she closed the door. As she turned to walk upstairs, she bumped into Kareem who was standing behind her, eavesdropping. "What are *you* doing, nosey?"

"Just listening, that's all. You know, that really *is* a good book. I read it a few years ago. I was kinda young at the time, so it took me a minute to get through it. I'd like to check it out again when you're finished with it, if you don't mind."

"Why don't I just give it to you now, and you can let me know how it was? Since it'll be your second time reading it, you should be able to give me some…how do you say it…oh yeah, *insight*."

"I'm not helping you, Pumpkin. He told *you* to read it. For once in your life, why don't you put your mind on accomplishing something on your own. If you pursue an education, it may keep those golden anklets off of you," he sarcastically stated as he pointed to the house arrest device she wore on her ankle.

"Whatever, nerd boy," she replied. As she began to walk upstairs, the doorbell rang again. "Damn, what does he want now," she asked herself as she opened the door. "Yes, Mr. Sim…"

"Mr. Sim? Is that how you speak to your auntie?"

"Tina!" she yelled as she hugged her. "How you been?"

"God's been good to me, girl. And you? I heard you had some court problems recently. Are you getting yourself together or what?'

"I'm working on it, Auntie. C'mon in and have a seat."

"Thanks. Where's your mom?"

"They didn't get home yet. If they're not here soon, I'm gonna go and throw something together for dinner."

"I tell you what. Why don't we go in the kitchen and do it together?"

"That sounds cool. Hey, what brings you here in the middle of the week anyway?" Katrina asked as they walked into the kitchen.

"Actually, I'm not the bringer of good tidings today. Sit down for a minute," she said as she grabbed Katrina's hand and escorted her into a seat at the table. "Your Auntie Michelle died in the hospital today of heart failure."

"What! How?"

"I don't know if your mother told you or not, but Michelle had AIDS."

"Who gave my aunt AIDS?" Katrina asked as she began to cry. "Why didn't anyone tell me?"

"I don't know. Maybe your mother didn't think you could handle it along with the fact she'd just had breast surgery. Maybe I shouldn't even be telling you this myself. I don't know. You just have to remember that it was her time to go."

"No, fuck that!"

"Pumpkin!" Tina shouted. "Your mouth!"

"I'm sorry, Auntie. I just can't accept the fact that it was her time to go. It should be that nigga's she was messing with time to go."

"No, Pumpkin," Tina said as she sat beside her and began to wipe her tears. "Michelle knew what she was doing, and I hate to say this but, the reality is, the dirt you do in the wash cycle comes out in the rinse. Your mother, Jackie, and I talked to Michelle for years about the way she was living. I'm not saying she knew her boyfriend had a disease, but she knew he was in the streets and that he used drugs, so that increased the probability of him contracting a disease."

"What kinda drugs? Weed?" Katrina nervously inquired.

"Among other things, I'm sure. From what I've heard, he's been seen buying heroin from time to time. All I know is that right now he's also in the hospital and he's on deck. In other words, his days are numbered."

"Good. He'd better be glad that God got to him before I did."

"Michelle always felt as if I hated her, but I didn't. I just hated her lifestyle." Tina's eyes became flooded. "Pumpkin, I visited her more than once while she was in the hospital and I watched as her body deteriorated with every visit. It killed me to watch such a loving person waste away. She had sores all over her face that wouldn't heal and she was always in excruciating pain. I wouldn't wish a death like that on my worse enemy. She did send a message for you, though."

"What's that?"

"She said for you to make sure you don't end up like her."

Katrina silently thought to herself. "I won't, Aunt Tina. I promise."

"Good. How's everything otherwise?" Tina asked as she got up and began looking through their cabinets for something to cook.

"Alright, I guess. I suppose you heard about my gang affiliations, huh?"

"Actually, I did. I was just waiting for you to tell me about it yourself."

"Well…"

"Wait, before you start, I thought *we* were cooking dinner together."

"Oh, my bad," she said as she stood up and began helping her search for pots. "Anyway, let's just say that I've done a lot of bad things I'm very sorry for and, from now on, I'm gonna try extremely hard to turn my life around."

"And what you just said shall suffice. I've never been the type of person to hold a grudge against someone for mistakes they've made, especially once they've repented for them. Just make sure you hold true to your word, and everyone will respect you. Your word is your bond. Never forget that."

"I won't, Auntie."

"What time does your mother usually come in? I know what I have to tell her is going to tear her apart. Oh, I forgot to tell you. Jackie's also coming by with her kids tonight, so we might want to make a little extra just in case."

"A little? Shoot, we might as well order out. I think five or six pies should be enough." Katrina looked at Tina and they both exploded with laughter.

"Everything's gonna work itself out, Pumpkin."

"I hope so." Katrina paused. "Aunt Tina?"

"Yes, honey?"

"I just have one question to ask you."

"What's that, Pumpkin?"

"I've never seen you with a man, and I doubt if you've ever taken care of one. You also don't have any children."

Tina stopped taking food from the cabinet and turned to face Katrina. "And your point is?" she asked.

"I was just wondering if you even know *how* to cook." Katrina stared at her with half a grin, trying to restrain her laughter.

"Whatever, girl! Pass the damn measuring cup," Tina said as she snatched a pot from Katrina.

# CHAPTER 25

## Kareem:
## 4-25-99

"Hey, Kareem, let me holla at you for a minute."

"Huh?" Kareem said as he turned around. "Oh, what's up, L? Listen, you gotta make it quick, man. I'm late for my next class."

"I hear you, homie. Have you seen your sister?"

"Nope. Last time I spoke to her was right before third period and she said she was on her way to graduation rehearsal. Do you want...hey, wait a minute. When did you get out?"

"I got out two days ago, lil' homie. What's up with you?"

"Still trying to finish up my education here and prepare for college, that's all. And you?"

"Still bangin', homie. That's why I'm looking for your sister. I hear she stepped down, dropped her flag. A lot of chicks she used to roll with wanna see her knocked off for that, and some rival bitches want to get at her for some o' the shit she did to them."

"Listen, L, my sister always kept me out of her street business. I *do* know that she's been home a lot more often than usual. She's been mentoring our little brother lately. She said she doesn't want him to grow up trying to be like her. My mom's also been sick lately, so Pumpkin has been taking up some of the slack until she gets better."

"That's cool, lil' homie, but if she dropped her flag, there ain't much I can do to protect her. You know what I'm sayin'? I just hope she still got her heat with her. I don't care what you decide to do with your life after you leave these streets, so long as you remember never to lay down your arms, you feelin' me? Sometimes, all the bullshit that you do catches up with you."

"Damn, that's the late bell. I gotta go. I'll tell Pumpkin that you were looking for her if I see her, okay?" Kareem extended his hand to offer Laurence a handshake. "Take care of yourself, L."

"No doubt, lil' homie. Dig, if you ever need anything, holla at me, ya hear? I still got your back."

"Absolutely, man. I'll see you later."

"Peace, lil' homie."

Terminologies such as "banging", "flag dropping", and "packing heat" are frequently heard in many urban and now, sometimes, suburban areas. "Banging" is short-term for gang banging, while "flag dropping" refers to those who put in for an early retirement from their particular organization. "Heat" is just another name for a gun.

Big L was back and bigger than ever, so to speak. Although he shed about forty or fifty pounds while he was away, his muscular composition gave the appearance of an addition of at least one hundred pounds of solid bulk.

Although he only served two years as junior executive at one of the prominent firms mentioned earlier, he was able to benefit from the use of such corporate facilities as the *"fitness center"* and *"dining lounge"*, thus shaping him into the man he was today: a massive, eighteen-year-old, tyrannical ruler.

Abraham Lincoln High School was not your average urban high school, but it was the only high school in the area. This caused a diverse mix of ethnicities to become overcrowded under one roof. The school was approximately fifty percent Black, thirty percent Latino, and fifteen percent White. The remaining five percent consisted of a combination of Asians and West Indians. You would think with such a cultural combination, racism would be a major issue. Actually, it wasn't. As times change, so do many ancient ideologies.

School ended at 2:50 p.m. and two things were always guaranteed: at least one altercation between students, and the presence of a minimum of ten police cars patrolling the high school.

"Pumpkin!" Kareem shouted across the street. "Pumpkin, wait up!"

Katrina sat on the hood of a car positioned across the street. She quickly flicked a cigarette she was smoking when she heard her brother shouting. "What?" she responded as he jogged toward her.

"Did you see Big L?"

"Big L?" she repeated. "He's home?"

"Yeah, somehow he got inside of the school and was looking for you. He said for you to catch up with him as soon as you can. Something about you dropping your flag?"

Katrina's heart palpitated upon hearing the news. She knew he wouldn't come after her, but she also knew he'd be infuriated, just as she would have been if the tables were turned.

"Whatever. I'll see him when I see him," she *boldly* stated. "Are you on your way home?" she asked.

"Not yet. I have to drop my report off to my English teacher first. Why?"

"I wanted to know if you could swing around the corner and meet Malcolm at the elementary school."

"No problem. Just give me about ten minutes or so, alright?"

"Cool, I appreciate it. I don't think it's a good time for him to be around me. I'll meet you at home later."

"Are you all right, Pumpkin? You look like something's bothering you."

"I'm straight. I just have to take care of some things, that's all."

"Well, let me know if you need me. I *am* your brother, you know."

"Yeah, I know."

As Kareem began to walk back toward the high school, a small group of Katrina's ex-coworkers headed her way.

"What's up y'all?" Katrina firmly asked.

"Nothing. What's up with you?" René responded.

Katrina's demeanor suddenly changed. She began to realize René's inquires concerning her well-being were actually counterfeit. This may have been evident from the way the rest of the girls positioned themselves around her. It was a classic ambush maneuver.

Katrina calmly leaned her back against the car to get a better view of the situation and slightly lifted her shirt to reveal the butt of her favorite sidekick. "Is there something y'all need or something one of you feels you need to hold?" she asked the astonished girls. Surprised by Katrina's defensive tactics, each of the girls took a step back.

"Naw, K.K., we were just checkin' on you, that's all," René stated.

"I'm cool," Katrina responded.

"Well, I guess we'll holla at you later."

"Yeah, I guess you will," she sarcastically replied as she lowered her shirt.

Katrina watched as her newly acquainted nemesis motioned her posse to follow her away from what almost turned out to be someone's ill fate. Although they had her outnumbered, they knew the casualties would not have been in their favor.

As Katrina began walking uphill and toward her neighborhood, she noticed the silhouette of a large-figured man standing against the horizon. She tried to focus her eyes to obtain a better analysis, but the glare of the sun made it nearly impossible. As her distance from the figured decreased, she began to realize who was waiting for her.

"Oh shit, L, what you doin' out here?"

"What's goin' on, K.K.?" he said as he offered their clandestine handshake. His hand appeared to be twice the size it was before he went to jail. It was obvious the time he spent in the juvenile detention center was well spent. As the sun shimmered against his massive arms, every muscular detail became more evident. The creases of his corn rows glistened as the end of each braid dangled near his shoulder blades. His outfit was nothing out of the ordinary, but the tight, white A-shirt, baggy jeans, and tan construction boots would have caused any woman of age to consider committing the crime of statutory rape. Up till now, neither of them ever really noticed how attractive the other had become. At this point, it didn't matter. The only problem was they knew their relationship was business and anything more was definitely out of the question.

"I saw what just happened down there," he added. "You know I..."

"It ain't nothin', big homie," she interjected. "I know the rules and I don't expect you to get involved with what's goin' on. I made my decision and, believe me, I'm ready to deal with the bullshit that follows. Feel me? When did you get out anyway?" she asked as she pulled a cigarette from her pocket and began searching for her lighter.

Laurence pulled a lighter from his back pocket and offered to light her cigarette. "I got home two days ago. I had to get everything straight with my probation officer before I could get out here and see you. What happened? Why'd you drop your flag? I feel a little disappointed 'cause I thought you would hold me down while I was away."

"It wasn't like that," she responded as they began to walk toward her house. "I had a lot of shit goin' on that started to change me. My mom's been sick. She just had surgery because of cancer, and I felt it was time to be a big sister to my little brother."

"Yeah, I heard about that from your other brother. I'm sorry 'bout your mom. Is she all right?"

"I don't know what's with her. She's been goin' back and forth to the hospital lately, but I think it's got to do with her aftercare. You know, 'cause of the surgery. Anyway, now I got these bitches thinkin' they gonna roll me out or somethin'. Fuck them hoes! I showed they asses how to bang, you feel me? How the fuck they think they gonna roll up on me without they heat? I shoulda shot René in her fuckin' face for even thinkin' 'bout trying to see me."

"Calm down, K.K. It ain't gonna get you nowhere

blackin' out like that. You see where I just came from. I ain't tryin' to see you there and neither is your little brother, you know what I'm sayin'?"

"Yeah, I feel you. It's just fucked up that not only do I have to worry 'bout them bitches from the other squads, I gotta worry 'bout my own, as well. How are you lookin' at me, L?"

"You know I always had love for you. I ain't tryin' to see nothin' happen to you, but I gotta figure out a way to have your back without gettin' involved. Maybe I can have some of the kings holla at them or something. Maybe I can get them to back down."

"Don't worry 'bout it, L. We can't let what I did cause you to get involved and appear weak, you know what I'm sayin'? Rules are rules. I got this shit, L. I created them bitches and I'll be their destruction if they fuck with me."

"I'm still gonna watch you, Pumpkin. I gotta do that, you know."

She stopped at the corner of her street, turned, and faced him. "I know, and I'd do the same for you."

Suddenly, a strange feeling seemed to crawl over her body. It began at her heart and spread throughout her body in the form of pimples. Laurence smiled and leaned forward to hug her. Somehow, during the embrace, their lips met and momentarily became locked. After a few seconds, they gently pulled away from each other and, with their eyes still closed, slowly swayed back and forth as if intoxicated.

"W-W-What the fuck was that?" she mumbled.

"I-I don't know," he said as he opened his eyes, "but I wish it hadn't ended."

"I, uh, I gotta go. I don't feel too good. Holla at me tomorrow," she slowly replied.

"Yeah, no doubt," he answered. "Tomorrow."

Katrina continued down the street and toward her house. The sick feeling she described sat deep within her stomach and almost made her want to vomit. She could not comprehend what just took place on the corner. This man, who she looked at as a brother all her life, just jettisoned her soul into heaven, and no matter how hard she tried, it felt impossible to return back to earth. Houston, we have a problem!

As Katrina approached her porch, she noticed her brothers sitting outside, attempting to enjoy the day's fresh, spring breeze.

"What the hell was that all about?" Kareem asked.

"Yeah, what the hell was that all about?" Malcolm repeated.

"Watch your mouth, Malcolm!" Katrina snapped. "And as for you, Mr. Nosey, mind you damn business."

"Yeah, mind your…"

"Malcolm!" she snapped.

"Sorry, Pumpkin," he said, lowering his head.

"Kareem, we're gonna have to watch how we speak around him from now on. He's startin' to pick up some of our bad habits."

"You're right, sis, my bad. Anyway, are you going to tell me who that was on the corner tongue wrestling with you or not?"

"It was L, alright!" she exclaimed as she stepped past them and attempted to quickly dart into the house.

"Laurence?" Kareem shouted. "Oh hell no, I want details." Kareem reached out, grabbed Katrina's wrist, and pulled her back outside. "When did all of this start? I thought you were a dyke all this time," he began to giggle.

An expression of love was written all over her face as she slowly returned to the porch. "C'mon, let me have it, sis," he commanded.

"It's nothing to explain. Shoot, *I* don't even know how it happened. What's funny is that for some reason, I'm really glad it did. You know, Kareem, up until that moment, I never looked at him like that before. And deep down inside, I don't think he ever looked at me like that, either. This is really crazy."

"Well, Pumpkin, he did just come home from jail. There's no tellin' *what* was on his mind," he jokingly stated as he leaned against his sister and began laughing. "He probably would have French kissed a baboon if he got too close to one.

"Get off of me, Kareem," she said as she pushed him. "You make me sick sometimes, I swear." She smiled as she jerked her wrist from his hand and stomped into the house.

Moments after Katrina stepped into the house, Corey's car pulled into the driveway. His tie was loosened and his appearance looked as if he was the sole survivor of a plane crash. His eyes were bloodshot red and very swollen.

"Daddy!" Malcolm shouted as he stood and ran down the stairs.

"Hey, Daddy, what's wrong?" Kareem asked.

"What's up, fellas," he said as he picked up Malcolm. "Where's your sister?"

"She just went inside."

"You guys come in for a minute. I need to talk to you. Katrina!" he shouted as he opened the screen door and stepped into the house. "Come downstairs for a minute."

"Comin', Daddy," she responded.

"Everybody sit down for a minute," he said as he

opened the refrigerator and grabbed a cold beer. "Listen, guys, your mother's in the hospital again. I'm not sure what's going on with her, but…oh, c'mon now, no crying," he pleaded as he fought to hold back his own tears. "We've got to be strong, fellas."

"Why, Daddy? Why is God doing this to her? She's not a bad person or anything. I don't understand," Kareem wept as he stood and ran to his room.

"Kareem!" Corey yelled.

By this time, Malcolm was crying so violently, he couldn't comprehend anything else his father said.

"I'll talk to Kareem later," Katrina interceded. "You know how close he is to Mommy. It's kinda hard for him to deal with everything that's happening to her."

"Thanks, Pumpkin. I've gotta get back to the hospital. I'll call you later tonight and check on you guys, alright?"

"Okay, Daddy. I love you. Be strong, alright?"

"Yeah," he said as he kissed her forehead. "Bye, honey. See you later, Malcolm."

"Bye, Daddy," Malcolm whimpered.

"C'mon, Malcolm, let's go upstairs and get freshened up," Katrina said as she wiped the tears from her eyes.

"Alright," he said.

# CHAPTER
# 26

"Hey, Denise, how are you feeling?" Corey whispered as he sat on the hospital bed beside his wife and held her hand.

"Not too well, honey," she slurred.

"What are the doctors saying?"

"They didn't get all of the cancer when they removed my breast and it spread to my brain. Don't cry, Corey. I'm not sad. I'm feeling really woozy right now because of the medication, but before I fall asleep, I wanna tell you something. First, I love you more than you could ever imagine. My life with you has been everything I ever wanted and more. I have absolutely no regrets. There *is* one thing that I need to say to you, and I don't want a response or an answer. Corey... I know about what happened between you and Kimberly, and I have ever since the day after it took place."

"Denise, I..."

"Don't say anything, Corey. Let me finish. Your so-called friend, Roman, told me. I know his plan was to hopefully get me into bed with his 'you can do better than him' story, but you know I'm not that type of woman. It didn't take much for me to see through the revenge in his eyes and figure out it must have been his lady that you slept with. It took me a long time to try and figure out what I did to deserve that from you, but after a while, I realized it wasn't me at all...it was you. It's also something you'll have to see

God about when it's your time. I do forgive you, Corey. I don't want you to think that I'm holding a grudge for what you did. Whether it was a mistake or not, I'm sure you had your reasons. There is one thing I want to apologize to you for, though…"

"Denise, you don't owe me anything."

"Yes I do, Corey. I apologize for not having my first child with you. You never said anything about it, but I know it crushed you when you found out. It was a mistake, Corey, and you know I would have never gotten an abortion. My mother raised me better than that."

Corey laid his head on the mattress and burst into tears. "I'm so sorry, Denise. I'm so sorry. Please forgive me. I know your illness is God's way of punishing me for what I've done. The sin I committed is coming back on me. I don't deserve you. That's why this is happening. Roman was right. You should have had better than me."

"Corey!" she yelled in a raspy tone. The strain on her vocal chords caused her to cough violently. "Don't ever let me hear you say his name or anything as ridiculous as that again. Do you understand me? What I am dealing with was written for me from birth. Nothing you could have done, or not done for that matter, would have made any difference. I never said my life was over. I just want you to face reality and recognize what's happening. I'm still in chemo and there's a chance I may pull through this successfully. I want you to be the man that I married and take charge of our family the way you always have and guide our babies, especially Kareem. He needs you more than the other two. He's exactly like me, so trust me on this one. He's always wanted a relationship with you and you never returned one to him. I'm sure you have your reasons, as you always do, but you're wrong on this one, Corey. Raise them to be better than us. Above everything else, stop blaming yourself for this. I forgave you years ago."

Corey lifted his head from the mattress and caught glimpse of Denise nodding off. As he wiped his tears, he still felt the need to apologize, but decided to let her rest instead. He knew she was right about everything she said except for one thing…he continued believing this was his punishment. He felt this way ever since she told him about her disease in their dining room. All he could do from that day until now was let it literally eat him alive on the inside. Sometimes he wondered if he would have confessed what he did would this still have happened to her. He knew it was true what she said about a person's life being written for them from birth and began wondering if that was why God put them together, because He knew someday Corey would commit the sin of adultery.

"Mr. Lambert. Mr. Lambert, wake up, please. I brought you a little snack. You've been here all evening without anything to eat," the nurse said as she handed him a doughnut and small cup of apple juice.

"Huh? Oh, thank you. I must have fallen asleep. What time is it?" he asked as he rubbed his eyes and observed the nurse checking his wife's vitals.

"It's 5:34 a.m.," she said as she placed a stethoscope on Denise's chest. She paused momentarily after checking her pupils and then faced Corey, "I'm sorry, Mr. Lambert, but I must ask you to step into the hallway for a moment."

"Why? What's wrong?"

"Please, sir, just step into the hallway. Thank you." As the nurse escorted Corey into the hallway, she began to summon a doctor for assistance. "Can someone get me a doctor, please!" she yelled.

Moments later, two doctors and a trio of nurses immediately hurried into Denise's room. Corey waited impatiently for someone to give him a heads up on the situation. Within ten minutes or so, one of the doctors stepped into the hallway and walked towards Corey.

"Mr. Lambert?"

"Yes, Doctor, I'm Mr. Lambert. What's wrong with my wife?"

"Sir, it is with deep sorrow that I must inform you that your wife has fallen into a coma."

"God, no," Corey replied as he fell back into his seat. "Please Lord, enough, enough," he mumbled to himself as he placed his head into his hands. "Take me instead. I can't bear going on without her."

"Mr. Lambert," the doctor consoled him as he placed his hand upon Corey's back, "go home and try to get some rest. There isn't much more you can do here. I'll contact you if there's any change in your wife's condition. Go to your children. They're going to need you now more than ever."

"Thank you, Doctor...?"

"Mitchell. Dr. Mitchell," he said as he extended his hand to Corey.

"Thank you, Dr. Mitchell. Please contact me immediately if there are any changes."

"I will. Goodnight, Mr. Lambert."

"Goodnight, Doctor," Corey said and began walking toward the elevator. As he waited for the elevator's arrival, he thought to himself and began to realize how much Denise and the doctor were right. It was time for him to be strong for his children. He took out his cell phone, called his job, and informed them he wouldn't be in that day.

As Corey entered his home, he continuously prayed over and over that it was all just a bad dream. That he'd wake up and his wife would be peacefully sleeping by his side as healthy and beautiful as the first night of their honeymoon. That next morning, he reminisced, was the greatest moment of his life. That morning was the birth of his bliss, a bliss which was sold at the price of a one-night stand.

He walked upstairs and lightly tapped on Katrina's door. "Pumpkin, are you awake?" he asked as he slowly pushed open her door.

"I am now, Daddy. What time is it?" she inquired while yawning. She focused on her father's face and began to worry. "What's wrong?" she asked as she sat up on her bed.

"You're the oldest, so I thought it might be best if I came to you first. Listen, your mother is in a coma."

"Oh no, Daddy! Do you think she'll come out of it?"

"I don't know. All we can do at this moment is pray." His lower lip quivered as he fought back his tears.

"It's gonna be all right, Daddy," she said as she reached forward and pulled him into her arms. Although he tried desperately to control his emotions in front of her, it was to no avail. He rested his head on her shoulder and quietly sobbed.

"Pumpkin, are you home yet?" Kareem shouted as he and Malcolm entered their hallway. "Malcolm, hang your jacket on the coat rack. Don't throw it on the floor like you always do. And take your book bag to the kitchen so you can start on your homework, okay?"

"Yup," he responded. "Kareem, sometimes you sound

just like Mommy."

"Whatever. Just meet me in the kitchen."

As Kareem entered the kitchen, he noticed his sister and father sitting at the dinner table.

"Hey, I didn't know you two were home. Why didn't you answer me, Pumpkin? I know you heard us come in." Kareem began to gradually become aware of the fact neither of them was paying attention to anything he was saying. "W-What's wrong?"

"Your mother passed away today, son. The doctors did all…"

Before Corey could finish his sentence, Kareem turned around, dashed out of the kitchen, and continued through the front door. He paused on the sidewalk in front of their home and raised his head toward the heavens. He closed his eyes to shield them from the sun as its rays glistened through his tears. After a few seconds, he turned to his left and began running full speed down his street, never stopping at the intersections. After walking another three or four miles, his path suddenly became a dead end. He realized he was back in his old neighborhood as he faced the entrance to the small park where Curtis had met his fate many years ago. He stopped walking momentarily before deciding to approach a group of kids which he recognized from school. They sat on the bleachers beside the basketball courts. He noticed they were engaged in sharing a couple cans of beer and passing a blunt back and forth. As he drew closer, one of them realized who he was.

"Damn, Kareem, what brings you here?"

"Just chillin', man. What's up with y'all? Matter of fact, what's up with one of those brews?"

"What? Since when did you start drinking? I always

thought you were the 'book man' on his way to college."

"Just pass me a fuckin' beer, nigga," he snapped, "and hurry up with that blunt."

The group of teens became frozen by Kareem's statement, but each of them knew better than to refuse his requests. This *was* Katrina's younger brother. At the same time, some of them wondered if she would come after them for getting her brother high and drunk. They all complied, but the wiser ones of the group decided they had enough and told Kareem he could have whatever was left as they stepped away from the awkward situation.

Kareem repeatedly inhaled, choked, and drank himself into a stupor. He became so blasted he didn't realize the sun had disappeared hours ago. Nor did he notice the large, blurred figure slowly approaching him. The man reached out, firmly grabbed a teen that was sitting beside Kareem, punched him in the face, and threw him so viciously that he nearly landed center court.

"What the fuck is y'all doin' to my lil' homie!" Laurence shouted. "Get the fuck outta here before I put some heat in one of y'all," he said as he pointed to those who still remained.

The teens scattered as they offered apologetic statements. Laurence climbed the stairs of the bleachers and sat beside Kareem who, at the moment, was having a very difficult time trying to sober up.

"Why you doin' this to yourself, homie? I heard about your moms, but this ain't how you need to do this. Y'all gotta come together right now. Your family is going crazy lookin' for your ass. When your sister called me, I figured you might be out here with these niggas tryin' to get fucked up. I probably would have done the same thing. But this ain't you, homie. Your family done came too far for you to throw that shit away, you feel me? How you think your mother's lookin' at you right now?"

Kareem struggled as he positioned himself in an upright position. After achieving his goal, the tears immediately followed.

"She was so good, L. Why did God have to take her from me? I don't understand this life shit, man. She did everything she was supposed to do, both as a mother and a wife. She cared about everyone. I feel like I don't know what to do anymore."

"Finish what she started, lil' homie. That's what you do, because that's what she would have wanted. I ain't sayin' it's gonna be easy, but after shit gets rough, it gets smooth again. That's the way I always look at it. At least you had a mother there for you. My mom was always too drunk to really pay me any attention and my pops stayed in jail. Your family is here for you. That's more than I can say for myself. And you know I got your back, so we're gonna get through this shit, alright?"

"Alright," he responded as he wiped his tears. "Yo, L, can you walk me home? I don't think I'm gonna make it."

Laurence became amused by Kareem's condition and began to laugh. "Yeah, c'mon, lil' homie," he said as he lifted Kareem from his seat.

"Oh, and thanks, L," Kareem said as he hugged him.

Kareem stumbled into his home and immediately came face to face with his father. It was difficult for him to decipher if the expression his father wore was one of fury or relief. Corey looked at his son, smiled, then turned and began walking upstairs to his bedroom. Kareem remained in the hallway and listened as his father's bedroom door squeaked before slowly becoming closed and locked. He began to realize that his father understood his reaction to the news of his mother's death and was just happy upon seeing his safe return. Kareem turned to face Laurence, who remained behind him on the front porch.

"Are you gonna come in?"

"I'm cool. Just tell your sister I'm out here for me."

"No problem, and hey, thanks again, L. Katrina! Laurence is outside," he shouted in the direction of her bedroom.

As Katrina walked downstairs, she became aware of her brother's condition.

"You've got to be fuckin' kidding me. You, of all people, went out and got blazed. How does it feel?"

"I think it's gonna be the first and last time it ever happens, so you'd better take a picture," he responded.

"How are you holding up?"

"I'm good, sis, thanks to Laurence." He stepped to the side to give Katrina a better view of his savior.

"Oh really? And what's it gonna cost me for my brother's safe return?" she asked as she pushed open the screen door and stepped onto the porch.

"Stop fuckin' with me, Pumpkin. I feel like it was my responsibility. I've known that lil' nigga damn near all my life, you feel me?"

"Yeah, I feel you. You wanna come in for a minute and get something to drink?"

"Naw, I just wanted to check on you, that's all. Are you straight?"

"Yeah, I guess. I just feel like I gotta be strong, that's all. You know, be the mother of the house now. It's strange, but what's really fucked up is that I knew after the first time I heard about her breast cancer that she wasn't gonna make it. That's part of the reason I decided to get off the streets."

"That's what I really wanted to talk to you about, but I wasn't sure if now was the right time to do it."

"It's cool. What's up, L?"

"I've been thinking 'bout what you said to me about leaving the street, and I respect it. Your life done changed over the years. You can't keep living like the rest of these niggas. I wish I could say the same for myself, but I know I ain't ever leaving this shit alone. It's all I know, feel me? The rest of them niggas that's still bangin' are just like me. They ain't got shit but their family in the streets. You were right. It was time for you to step down. Your family needs you and I'm gonna leave you to handle your business."

"What the fuck you mean 'leave me'?"

"Exactly what I said, Pumpkin, I gotta stop messin' with you. Our lives are gonna be different now and I don't wanna fuck yours up. Don't get me wrong. I love you and I'll always be here when you need me, but you know this shit ain't gonna be fair to either one of us."

"I don't know, L. Maybe you're right. I thought about the same thing after we kissed. I don't know where the fuck that shit came from. Maybe it's just something that built up in us over the years. I do wanna say one thing, though. If you ever decide to drop your flag, the first home you go to had better be mine. Now, you feel me?" she said as she smiled at him.

"No doubt, K.K....uh, excuse me, Katrina," he replied. "And another thing, as far as the kings and queens are concerned, you're safe. I thought to myself, 'Shit, I run this motherfuckin' town.' I made the rules and I'll break 'em.

The old heads know it and the lil' niggas fear questioning it. I know my pops had a lot to do with my reign, since he was the man before he went down. But now I got this shit. You just make sure you never lay down your heat, you feel me? It's still a lot of motherfuckers out here I don't trust and a few rival gangs I don't have any control over, alright?"

"Don't worry 'bout that. Just because I dropped my flag don't mean I turned stupid. You just be careful your damn self. Like you said, there's a lot of rival gangs out here that you don't have any control over."

"I got you. Keep your head up, alright?"

"I will. Hey, before you bounce, can I have another one of those kisses?" she shyly asked as she looked at the floor of the porch.

"Anytime you want one, Pumpkin." He leaned forward and gently, yet passionately, kissed her goodnight.

# CHAPTER
# 27

$\mathcal{T}$he following day, their home quickly became overcrowded with family members, close friends, and others who came to express their condolences and offer help with funeral arrangements. Kareem, who was still slightly hung-over, and his sister scurried back and forth while trying to smile and be as hospitable as possible during their rough times. Katrina continuously questioned her father and Malcolm concerning their wellbeing. There *was* one other person who she wasn't sure of that day: her grandmother. She listened as Diana repeatedly expressed how mothers should not have to bury their children, which was frequently contradicted with statements of "it was her time to go" and "at least she's in a better place now". For many people Katrina's age, this day would have been too overwhelming to handle, but amazingly, she continued to do an excellent job in holding herself together. Her strength was drawn from the fact that she constantly told herself she had to take her mother's place and make sure Malcolm grew to be a successful young man.

"Hey, Pumpkin, how are you holding up?" Tina asked as she placed her arm over her shoulder.

"Hey, Auntie, I'm fine. How 'bout you?"

"Between you and me, I'm in a lot of pain right now. I don't even know how I'm still standing. Every time I think about my sister, I become nauseous and lightheaded. I want to be strong for you guys, though," she said as she began to shed tears. "I just don't know what else to do, Pumpkin."

"Well, why don't you try doing like me?"

"And what's that?" she asked while reaching for a box of tissue which sat on a table.

"Be what she would have wanted you to be if she was still here: an excellent, supportive sister and aunt to her children. That's what I'm doing."

"What? You're being an aunt to her children," she laughed.

"You know what I mean, Auntie. Be strong. You always have been."

"Wow, who would have ever thought you'd be lecturing me on how to be strong. Listen, I've been thinking about asking you something for the past few weeks. Actually, it's more like an offer than a question."

"What's up?"

"I have a position available at the firm. It starts in the mailroom, but there's plenty of room for advancement with a lot of hard work and dedication. That is, if you're interested."

"Are you fuck...excuse me...are you playing with me?! Of course, I'm interested. When can I start?"

"As soon as you graduate from high school, honey. That should be in about a month or two, correct?"

"Yup," Katrina confirmed, "in June as a matter of fact. I don't believe this. One minute I'm running the streets, and the next, I'm given the opportunity to work for a law firm."

"We also provide scholarships to children we think deserve them. But I'm sure you already know who's on that list, right?" she said as she winked at her.

"Thanks, Auntie. I love you."

"I love you, too, Katrina. Let me go and check on

hugged her. She giggled as he carried her upstairs. "C'mon, let's go and steal some of Malcolm's toys," he whispered.

Corey stepped into the hallway and held Katrina's hand. "Are you okay, Pumpkin?"

"I'm fine, Dad. And you?"

"Much better now that I see my children are able to deal with this situation. Have you spoken to Malcolm?"

"Yeah, he's fine. One minute he's sitting down crying, and the next, he's running around the house. I guess you can say he's behaving like everyone else here."

"Yeah, you're right."

As Corey turned to walk into the kitchen, the doorbell rang.

"I got it, Daddy," Katrina stated.

"That's all right, Pumpkin. Go and check on your grandmother. I'll get the door," he said, walking toward it.

"Hey...Laurence, right?" Corey asked as he pushed the screen door open.

"Yes. How are you, Mr. Lambert?" he replied as he entered.

"I'm fine. Thanks for coming by." Just as Corey was about to shut the door, he noticed Roman walking up his stairs. Corey quickly stepped onto the porch and closed the door behind him. "I appreciate you coming by to pay your respects, but you're not welcome here."

Roman paused a step's distance from where Corey stood, astonished by his statement. "What are you talkin' bout, Corey? Why would you say something like that?"

That was the last thing Roman remembered saying. The next person he saw was standing over him on the sidewalk, asking him if he was all right. It didn't take much for him to realize Denise must have informed her husband of his advancements towards her. This was immediately followed by the assumption he was most likely unemployed as of that day.

Corey stepped into the bathroom located in the hall of the first floor and quickly ran cold water over his knuckles. As he exited, he was greeted by a long-time friend.

"C-money, how are you holding up?" Gary asked as he hugged him. "I'm so sorry about your loss, man. If there's anything I can do to help you through this, please call me."

"Thanks, Gary, I really appreciate the offer. The only thing is you repaid me a few years ago when you helped my daughter get off the streets. I never really got the chance to thank you for that. I also want to commend you on your success. It's funny, but I can vividly remember the day you stood on my porch and promised you'd get yourself together. It seems like only yesterday."

"Yeah, tell me about it, man. I see you've got a couple of grays coming in that beard of yours."

"Ha, I know you're not talking. Your hairline doesn't have anymore room left to recede."

"You know, it seems like the only one who *hasn't* aged is Momma Di. I spoke to her in the living room and, of course, she had absolutely no idea who I was. After I began to describe a scrawny, dirty young man who stood in front of the liquor store and helped her with her groceries, she stood up, hugged me, and burst into tears. All she continued to say after that was 'praise the Lord'."

"Yeah, that sounds like Momma Di alright. Listen, let me finish making my rounds and hopefully, when this is over, you and I can get together and catch up on old times."

"That sounds great, Corey. I see Katrina standing over there. Let me go and check on my prodigy."

"Alright, Gary. Give me a call in a couple of days and maybe we'll hook up."

"I will, Corey," he said as he shook his hand.

As Corey walked away, someone lightly tapped him on his shoulder. "Hi, Mr. Lambert."

Corey turned and was surprised by the sight of the young lady who stood before him. "Aw man, Brenda, I'm so happy to see you. How have you been?"

"I've been great, Mr. Lambert. This is my husband Charles and my daughter Yvonne."

"Husband and daughter? Has it been that long?"

"Pretty much," she replied.

"So what's been going on with you? I can't believe how you've matured. Last time I saw you, you were a skinny little nerd wearing glasses that were bigger than your face."

"Real funny, Mr. Lambert. Not in front of my husband, please," she jokingly requested.

"I'm sorry," Corey said as he extended his hand to greet her husband. "Where are my manners? It's just that I've known this kid for so long. She's like a daughter to me. She used to baby sit my kids for me years ago. It's hard for me to look at her like this."

"I understand, sir," Charles replied.

"Please, call me Corey. Listen, you guys make yourselves at home. Hey, how old is your baby?"

"She'll be five months next week."

"Wow, look how time flies. Well, I have to keep it moving. Brenda, make sure you exchange numbers with Katrina before you leave. She's been doing pretty well for herself and I'm sure she would love to talk to you, okay?"

"I will. I'll talk to you before we leave, Mr. Lambert."

"Make sure you do. It was nice meeting you, Charles."

"Same here, Corey," he said as he shook his hand.

Kareem remained in his room even after his newfound cousin became bored with him and decided to return downstairs to the action. He realized he felt more comfortable mourning alone. He pulled a notebook from his bookshelf, opened it, and wrote the title "My Ten Year Plan" at the top of the page. He then began to write a chronological list of steps he'd accomplish over the next few years that would lead to his success. Halfway down the page, he decided to go back and write "Mommy's Wish List" in parentheses underneath the title.

# CHAPTER 28

## Malcolm:
## 6-18-2002

"*K*atrina, you're wanted upstairs again! It's probably your *'Auntie'* summoning, as usual," her supervisor sarcastically informed her. "Take your time, kid. I don't want any problems."

"Thanks, Mr. Mitchell. I'll try not to be too long," Katrina responded as she stepped from her cubical.

Nearly three years had passed since Katrina's first day on the job and, just as Tina expected, she'd come a long way. Her term in the mailroom was short lived and she now worked as a file clerk on the fourteenth floor of the prestigious Blackwood Towers located in the center of the metropolis.

She stepped from the elevator on the 57th floor and was immediately greeted by a receptionist positioned across from the elevators.

"Good afternoon, Ms. Lambert. Your aunt is waiting for you in her office. And let me be the first to congratulate you on your success."

"What success?" Katrina asked, stunned by the

receptionist's comment.

"Oh, you haven't heard yet? Well, I won't be the one to spoil the surprise. Go ahead. Your aunt is waiting."

Katrina continued down the hall and toward Tina's office. As she entered, she watched as Tina stood in front of a large floor-to-ceiling window, admiring the city.

"Isn't it a beautiful day, Pumpkin?" she said as she turned around.

"Uh, I guess. There aren't any windows where I sit. You know, I've been in your office a hundred times and I still can't get over how huge it is. I'm so proud of you, Auntie. You've come a long way. I hope someday I can achieve what you have and get a corner office at a prominent law firm."

"And when you get there, you'll realize it's your accomplishments and not your office that you'll be proud of. That is a bad outfit you're wearing, Pumpkin. Where'd you get it?"

Katrina quickly looked down and glanced at the blue, pinstriped business suit and high heels she was wearing. Ever since her first day with the firm, she made it a point to dress her best. She even began wearing makeup and kept her hair looking beautiful at all times. Today, she decided to go with the "Farah Fawcett" look and flip the tips of her long, black hair outward.

"I picked this up at the mall," she replied while blushing. "I can't remember the name of the store, though."

"Are you sure you can't remember, or is it the fact that you don't want to give away your secret?" Tina laughed as she sat behind her huge, cherry wood desk. "Sit down for a minute," she requested. "I want to talk to you."

"Does this have anything to do with what the girl at the front desk was congratulating me about?" Katrina asked as she sat across from her.

"Who? Maria? She doesn't know what she's talking about. So how's your family doing? I haven't heard from anyone in a while."

"They're great. Kareem is getting ready for graduation. You know he's been accepted to Harvard. Dad's still running the trucking company, and Malcolm's doing pretty well in school."

"That's good. Tell your father to call me sometime. Tell him I said I'm still his sister, you know."

"I will. So what's this about?"

"Well, I wanted to know if you wanted to have lunch with me today. I know a beautiful restaurant with sidewalk seating. It's such a lovely day, I figured we should take advantage of it."

"I'd love to, but I need to inform my supervisor first."

"Don't worry about it. I'll call downstairs and let them know you'll be returning late from lunch."

"No, Aunt Tina, I need to be responsible for my own job. He already teases me whenever you need to see me. Let me do this, please," she requested.

Tina looked at Katrina and smiled. An expression of satisfaction was written all over her face. "I am so proud of who you've become, Pumpkin. And your mother would have been, as well. Go ahead downstairs and inform, excuse me, request a late lunch from your supervisor, and if everything is okay, meet me at my car. I'm parked in the garage."

"Thanks for understanding, Auntie."

As Katrina approached Tina's car, she noticed she was patiently leaning against the trunk. "Is everything all right?"

she asked.

"Yeah, I just thought it might be better if we walked to the restaurant. It's only about seven or eight blocks from here, and there's not a cloud in the sky."

"That's cool with me. All I know is I'm starving right now. I don't care how we get there."

As Tina and Katrina slowly strolled along the sidewalks of downtown, they peeked through storefront windows and discussed the array of outfits which donned the many mannequins. Upon reaching their destination, Tina was immediately greeted by one of the waitresses.

"Good afternoon, Ms. Banks. Will you be having the usual?"

"Yes, and a soda for my niece, please," she requested.

"A soda? Are you serious? I'll take a rum and coke, thank you." As the waitress walked away, she turned to Tina, who was shocked by her order. "Did you forget how old I am, Auntie? I *am* twenty-one now, and I'm sure I already told you that I've been drinking ever since I was thirteen."

"I'm sorry, sweetheart. I still look at you as my little Pumpkin. And looking at you today makes me forget that you used to be known as *Ms. Soprano* at one time. Which reminds me, how do you feel about going to college?"

Katrina's jaw fell to the table. "I-I've always dreamed of it, but never thought I'd see it. Why?"

"Well, the firm has decided to offer you a scholarship."

"Oh my God!" Katrina shouted as she placed her hands over her heart. "Thank you, Auntie! Thank you so much!"

"No, Pumpkin, thank yourself. It was your hard work

at the firm that earned you the scholarship. Along with the scholarship, there's a junior executive position you must fill. Don't think I influenced their decision. No one has *that* kind of power. Not myself or my partners."

"Really? I won't let you down, Auntie. I promise."

"Don't worry about me, Pumpkin. Just make sure you don't let yourself down. Again, I am sooo proud of you, and I know Denise is smiling down from heaven at this moment."

"Yeah," Katrina smiled. "Here's to my future," Katrina said as she raised her glass.

"To your future, honey," Tina agreed as she raised hers.

Two hours and four mixed drinks later, Tina glanced at her watch and realized what time it was. "Oh my goodness, you are so late."

"Really? What time is it?"

"It's almost two o'clock. Why don't you take the rest of the afternoon off? I'll let Mr. Mitchell know you won't be returning."

"Are you sure?"

"Well, if you're half as tipsy as I am, I think it would better if you went home. I'll catch a cab back to the office. Call it a reward for your promotion."

"I'm fine, Auntie. Actually, I don't feel a thing, but I could use a day off."

"Great. Then I'll see you in my office first thing in the morning to discuss everything in detail."

"I'll be there, and thanks for lunch, Aunt Tina. The next one's on me." She smiled as she stood from the table.

"You're damn right the next one's on you, with the money you'll soon be bringing in," Tina responded as she stood and stuck out her arm for a cab. "How are you getting home?"

"I'm gonna walk and catch some fresh air. Malcolm gets out of school soon, so maybe I'll surprise him by meeting him there."

"Are you sure?"

"Yeah, I'm fine. I'll see you in the morning," Katrina said as she began to walk down the street. Her thoughts suddenly shifted to Laurence, and she began to wish his life was changing for the better, just as hers was beginning to.

By the time Katrina reached Malcolm's school, the students were being dismissed. She looked around the playground and attempted to locate her brother. To her surprise, he located her first.

"Pumpkin!" he yelled as he ran towards her. "What are you doing here?"

"I thought you might be in the mood for some ice cream or something. What do you think?"

"How 'bout some candy?"

"Whatever you want. It's on me, Mal," she said while lightly pinching his cheek.

They left the playground and began walking home. Malcolm looked up and noticed Katrina smiling. "What are you so happy about?" he asked.

"Everything. I'm just having a wonderful day. It's not too hot or too cold, there's not a cloud in the sky, I have my favorite person in the world with me and I got a promotion today."

"Wow! You got a promotion? I'm so happy for you, Pumpkin. Like I told you before, I want to be like you when I get older. That's why I work so hard in school. You know what else I want?"

"What's that, Mal?"

"I want to be famous like you, too."

Katrina abruptly stopped walking, faced her brother, and dropped to one knee. "That's not what you want, and don't ever let me hear you say that again! Do you understand me? I thought that was what I wanted when I was little, and it got me nowhere. What you want is to be a successful young man when you get older. That's what I want and that's what Mommy would have wanted if she were alive. Don't let these streets, or what's in them, ever prevent you from achieving that. Do you hear me?"

"Yeah, I understand."

"Good. Now what do you want to eat?" she asked as she stood to her feet.

"I want some candy, chips, and soda!"

"Damn, ain't you the hungry one. I guess you earned it since you *are* at the top of your class. C'mon, we'll go to the bodega around the corner."

As they approached the store, Katrina noticed the vegetable and fruit stands that surrounded the perimeter and decided to make a celebration dinner for her family. She let Malcolm step inside and pick out what he wanted while she remained behind and sampled the different vegetables on display. The heat from the sun delivered a spine tingling sensation to the back of her neck. She began to feel as if it were her mother smiling down on her.

"Well, well, well…if it isn't the notorious K.K. gracing us with her presence this beautiful spring day. Long time no see. Ooh, I see we're Ms. Successful now, huh?"

Katrina immediately dropped a tomato she was in the process of testing for freshness and turned to face the female who taunted her. "Excuse me? I don't think I know yo' ass."

"Well, let me refresh your memory," the stranger sarcastically said as she looked at her minions. "Let us think back for a minute to an abandoned building you were in years ago. I believe it was a jump in that was taking place."

Katrina knew exactly what the girl spoke of, but couldn't place the young lady's face. She was too young to have been one of *her* rivals, but the bandana hanging from her back pocket made one thing obvious: she was definitely a banger. Katrina quickly realized she was outnumbered and decided to casually make her way inside of the store. As she backed inside, a voice repeatedly echoed in her head, *"... never lay down your heat, you feel me?"*

*"Shit, where's Malcolm?"* she thought to herself.

"I don't think I know y'all bitches, and if you knew who you were fuckin' with, you'd bounce outta here while you still got a chance," Katrina advised as she looked for a weapon.

"Fuck you, bitch! We know all about you, K.O.K. and K.O.Q. Fuck all y'all motherfuckers!"

"What's wrong, Pumpkin?" Malcolm asked as he slowly walked toward his sister.

Katrina never took her eyes away from the group of girls that slowly walked inside the store.

The owner of the store, who stood behind a cash register, quickly realized what was happening and decided to push a silent alarm button located under the machine. "I think it's time for you young ladies to leave my store," he commanded.

"Fuck you, papi! BLACK WIDOWS, BITCH!" the girl shouted as she pulled a .25 caliber automatic from her hip and fired three shots.

Katrina immediately reacted and pushed her brother

into a cart filled with various fruit. She then dove behind a rack filled with bags of chips. She tightly shut her eyes as she listened to one of the bullets whiz past her left ear. The bags of chips exploded overhead as she fell to the floor. Just as quickly as the young girl yelled the name of her clique, the chaos seemed to cease through the bodega.

Katrina laid motionless waiting for the heat of the slug's entry to commence burning her flesh before deciding to stand to her feet. She glanced across the store and saw that her brother was still ducking behind the fruit stand which had collapsed and partially rested against his back. After hearing the group of sirens approaching in the distance, she slowly stood to her feet and began walking to him.

"Malcolm," she whispered. "Malcolm, are you all right?"

She saw he wasn't moving and knew the shock of the situation must have frozen him. "Aw man, Daddy's gonna have a fit when he sees your clothes. You got juice all over you. Malcolm." As Katrina drew closer, she realized it wasn't juice on him at all. It was blood. "Malcolm!"

Katrina rushed to her brother, rolled him on his back, and immediately noticed a hole which sat in his left breast. He was no longer breathing.

Darkness surrounded her as she dropped to her knees, pulled him to her bosom, and cradled him. A tear never dropped from her eyes. The only tears were those of an unpredicted rainstorm as it began to crash against the pavement outside of the store.

Her arms collapsed to her sides as a police officer gently pulled her baby brother from her grasp. "Are you alright, Miss?" another officer asked as he kneeled by her side. The officer's words were muffled and Katrina had no desire, nor energy to respond.

Katrina knew why this happened. She only wished it was her that it happened to. For years, the death of the girl she murdered haunted her and, although it was a mistake, she knew it would come back on her sooner or later. She never thought it would be through the one person who meant the world to her: Malcolm. She never really mourned the loss of her mother. She accepted it as it was just her time to go. She figured her mother lived a beautiful, productive life and had no regrets when the Lord called for her return. Her decease strengthened her and made her into the woman she was today. Malcolm's death, on the other hand, delivered a catastrophic blow and she knew it would be nearly impossible to rebound from it.

Twenty minutes later, Katrina watched as two paramedics covered Malcolm's face with a sheet, strapped him to a gurney, and lifted him into the back of an ambulance. A crowd began to blanket the entrance of the store as another paramedic pulled Katrina to her feet and escorted her through the curious horde of bystanders. Most of the faces, who silently asked if she was okay, were very familiar to her. Katrina heard nothing but a deafening ring in her ears and her vision remained slightly blurred.

The rain gradually eased, and the rays of the sun peeking through the clouds caused Katrina to wonder if they were angels ushering her brother's soul to the heavens. Tears finally began to fill her eyes.

Suddenly, her silence was broken by a proverbial voice. "Pumpkin! Pumpkin, where are you?!"

Laurence forced his way through the crowd and embraced Katrina. "Are you all right, baby?" he asked, clutching her tightly.

"Excuse me, young man, you're in the way. I need you to step back while we examine her," a paramedic requested.

"It's okay. He's my best friend," she informed him.

"Pumpkin, some of my people just told me what happened. Are you shot?"

"No, I'm okay, L. They took my little brother," she said as she burst into tears. "Those bitches shot him, L. They killed him."

"Are you her boyfriend?" a detective asked.

"No, officer, we're best friends."

"Well, I can see from your tattoos that you're affiliated with the Knockout Kings, is that correct?"

"Yes," Laurence answered.

"I thought so. Is this a gang related incident?" he asked while looking at Katrina.

"No, officer," she responded, "they were trying to rob me."

"Listen, I don't think right now is a good time for questioning, but here's my card. I want you to contact me at the precinct as soon as possible. There are a few things I would like to discuss with you. You know, it's funny." He paused. "The store owner said the suspects were definitely part of the Black Widows, and my partner just informed me that he rounded up most of them not far from this location. The crazy thing is that their leader is nowhere to be found. You wouldn't happen to know anything about that now, would you, Mr. Knockout?" he said, staring at Laurence.

"No, officer, I was in the barbershop when someone busted in and told everyone what had happened."

"In the barbershop with braids, huh?" the detective said as he stepped closer to Laurence.

"Yes. I was waiting to get my beard trimmed up."

"If you say so, young man. As I said, ma'am, you can contact me as soon as you feel a little better. Thank you for your time," he said as he walked away.

"Why don't you go home and get some rest, Miss," the paramedic insisted.

"I'll take her," Laurence interceded.

"Thanks, L," Katrina said as she stood from the edge of the rear of the ambulance.

As Katrina and Laurence slowly walked to her home, Laurence patiently waited for her to speak. After traveling a few blocks, he realized she had nothing to say, so he decided to let her in on his little secret.

"You know I got that lil' bitch stashed in a basement right now."

"What? What did you say?"

"The lil' girl that kill your brother...my people got her stashed in a basement right now. Right before I got to the store, my man called me on my cell and told me they had just burned one of her eyes out with a soldering iron to get information from her. She sang like a canary. He told me she said something about being the younger sister of some bitch you killed a couple of years ago. I wasn't trying to hear shit he said. I told him to hold her ass there until I spoke to you. You know, these lil' kids got some nerve trying to attack us. Who the fuck do they think they are? Anyway, what you wanna do?"

"Let her go."

"What! That bitch just killed your bro..."

"Let her go, L," she repeated calmly. "My past came back on me."

"Are you sure?"

"Yes, I'm sure. I'm just not sure how I'm going to tell

my family Malcolm's been killed."

"I'm surprised at you, Pumpkin. But, more than that, I'm proud of you. The chick I grew up with would have gone to that basement and shot the bitch in the face. I'll call my man and tell him to release her, if that's what you want. She'll be too afraid to talk to the police, and her missing eye will just have to be a gift from me for *my* loss, you feel me?"

Katrina paused and faced Laurence. "Thanks, L. Listen, I'll be okay. I just need to walk by myself for a while."

"I feel you. If you need me, call me," he said before gently kissing her forehead.

"I will," she assured him.

Katrina watched as Laurence slowly disappeared beyond the horizon. She looked up and observed a bird feeding its young. *"Life's not over,"* she thought to herself as she continued home.

# Corey:
# End/Beginning

# (6 mos. Later)

*C*orey sat in his favorite chair and stared at a family portrait which sat on the mantle above his fireplace. The portrait was surrounded by various memorabilia which told stories of the many accomplishments of the Lambert family: Kareem's trophies for academic achievements, Katrina's high school diploma, and Denise's Bachelors degree to name a few.

*"I wouldn't change any of it for the world,"* he thought to himself as he took another sip of cognac from his glass. The alcohol caused him to drift in and out of reality as he reminisced over the times he shared with his wife and the time he wished he could have spent with his son.

After Malcolm's death, the living room became his favorite place. It was unbearable for him to occupy his bedroom, and every time he passed his son's room, he would become so lightheaded, he'd nearly collapse. Today was six months to the day since the murder of his son, and six months to the day, he mourned his death while sitting in the same seat.

Corey's depression began to affect his appearance. His beard had become full and unkempt as the gray intertwined with the darker hair. His co-workers and subordinates noticed the difference, but no one was able to come up with a solution to his problems. What *do* you tell a man who just lost his wife and youngest child in less than a four year span? Nothing.

As Corey continued to sit and drown himself in Hennessy, Kareem quietly walked into the living room, dropped his book bag, and began stomping snow from his boots in an attempt to jolt his father back to life.

"Whoa!" Corey shouted as he sat up. "Oh…hey, son. Listen, have a seat. There's something I've wanted to talk to you about."

"Good, Dad, because there's something I've been wanting to talk to you about, as well."

"Great. Then we're on the same page. That's a good start," Corey responded in a drunken tone. "Why don't you go first, son."

"It's you, Dad," Kareem said as he sat across from his father. "Look at you! You're wasting away. You don't speak to me and Pumpkin anymore. You always look as if you haven't had a bath in weeks, and you're always drunk! How the hell do you expect Pumpkin and me to get through this when you're showing us the best way to get through this is to give up? What happened to Mommy and Malcolm happened. There's nothing we can do to change that. But damn, Daddy, we still have to be a fuckin' family!" he shouted as his eyes began to swell.

"Hey, hey, son, there's no need for that kind of language," Corey said as he tried to focus on his son. "You're right, though. You're absolutely right. I gotta get off my ass and finish what I started. I need to be a father to you guys. I'm sorry," he apologized as he placed his glass on the coffee table.

"It's okay, Dad. Just come back to us," Kareem pleaded as he stood up, walked to his father, and sat beside him.

Corey placed his hand on Kareem's lap. "Listen, son, I owe you a major apology…an apology that I don't owe to anyone but you."

"What are you talking about?" Kareem inquired.

"Our relationship. It's been shitty ever since you were born, and it's all my fault. I'm gonna speak to you man-to-man for a moment, so if I curse, please forgive me. It's not to disrespect you."

"Okay."

"I'm sure you know by now that Katrina is not my biological daughter."

"Yeah, and?"

"Part of that falls on the reason our relationship is the way it is."

"I don't understand."

"Your mother and I fell in love with each other at a very young age and we made a promise to get married as soon as we were old enough to. Obviously, we did, but there was one addition to the equation: Katrina. I accepted Katrina from the first time I laid eyes on her and vowed to raise her as my daughter. I was assured that her father was out of the picture and would never return. That bitch ass nigga wouldn't even man up to his responsibilities. Anyway, time passed and not only did my love for your mother grow, but so did my love for Katrina. So much so, I couldn't deal with the fact that I wasn't her real father. I began to want that more than anything in the world. For some reason, I felt if she was, our bond as a family would have been tighter. When you were born, I was proud to have you as my first child. As time passed, it became harder and harder to face the fact that you were my first child, but not your mother's."

Corey watched as Kareem's head dropped and tears poured from his eyes.

"Don't cry, son," Corey said as he began to also shed tears. "It's not you. It's me. I've wasted your entire childhood hating something you had no control over and I'm sorry. You've always been the son that I wanted and I want to spend the rest of my life trying to be the father you've always deserved. I'm proud of the man you've become and I love you with all my heart, son. I only wish I could have been a better father than I was when you needed me the most. Please forgive me."

Corey stood from his seat to walk toward the hallway. Before he stepped past his son, Kareem sprung from his seat and blocked his path. They faced each other momentarily. Suddenly, Kareem reached out and forcefully pulled his father into his arms. Corey wept as he slowly raised his arms and embraced his son.

"I forgive you, Daddy," Kareem cried.

As they tightly clinched to each other, Katrina entered the house and walked past the living room.

"Am I missing something here?" she asked as she placed her briefcase on the floor.

"Yeah, a hug," Corey said as he opened an arm to her.

"Good. I need one of those right about now," she said as she entered the living room.

As Corey released his grip from his children, the

phone in the kitchen began to ring.

"I'll get that," he said, walking into the kitchen.

"Hello?"

*"Hi, may I speak to Corey?"*

"Speaking. Who is this?"

*"Oh, you don't remember my voice now?"*

"C'mon, I don't have time for games. Who's speaking?"

*"This is Kimberly. How've you been?"*

"Well, long time no hear. What made you call me?"

*"Actually, I just wanted to send my deepest condolences. I heard about what happened to your wife. I'm so sorry, Corey. How are you holding up?"*

"I'm pulling through. How did you find out?"

*"I still have friends back home, of course. How are your children doing?"*

"They're fine. We just lost Malcolm recently, so we're trying to get through that."

*"Oh my God, you've got to be kidding me! What happened?"*

"It's a long story. I'd rather not get into it."

*"Are you guys all right?"*

"We will be. We're just taking it one step at a time. How's everything been with you?"

*"Well, my career has taken off since I left, and I'm still single, of course. But I'm sure you would have already figured that much out."*

"To be honest with you, I haven't given it much thought. Well, thanks for calling, Kim, and I wish you much success in your endeavors."

*"Thank you, Corey, and the same goes for you."*

"Listen, Kim, I just have one last question before we hang up. What ever happened…?"

*"I know what you're wondering, Corey, and the answer is no. I'm just doin' me right now, alright?"*

"Okay, well, thanks for checking in and please feel free to stay in contact, alright?"

*"I will, Corey. Darn, I have to go. Take care of the family you have left, you hear me?"* Kimberly rushed to finish their conversation.

"I will, Kim. Goodbye."

*"Goodbye, Corey."*

As Kimberly hung up the phone, Corey heard the voice of a young child begin to speak in the background. ***"Mommy, can you help me…"***

•  •  •  •  •

This is the story of the Lambert family that has shaped me into the successful woman I have become today. They consist of events that have been passed down to me from my father, combined with experiences I have faced personally. If there is one thing I hope people draw from this, it's to understand the value of the family that God has blessed you with.

Thank you,
*Katrina 'Pumpkin' Lambert*

# Acknowledgments

First, I would like to say all praise is due to the Most High; The Most Beneficent, The Most Merciful.

Secondly, I want to thank my parents for their upbringing, love, patience, and continous motivation. They are the true inspiration which drives me to contiue writing. Next I want to extend my love and thanks to everyone who is part of the Sabuur family by sending them one message: A chain is only as strong as its weakest link. If we remember that, this family can achieve anything it wants. Finally, I thank my true friends, (you know who you are). You've been there for me since the beginning, and I'll be there for you until the end.

# DEBORAH SMITH PUBLICATIONS

"THE BEST IN URBAN,
CHRISTIAN &
GENERAL FICTION"